Encounter at
Salvation Creek

When rich young Englishman, Born Gallant, arrives in
America after the death of his father, he goes first to see
family friend William Pinkerton. The boss of the famous
detective agency at once gives him an assignment: the head of
the Kansas City office has been murdered, there has been an
attempt on Pinkerton's life, and he wants to know why.

From that day on, Gallant finds himself embroiled in a
fight to the death against gunmen hired by warring cattlemen
fighting against reorganization of their industry. Helped by
young trainee lawyer, Melody Lake, and newspaperman, Stick
McCrae, Gallant's fight to bring the killers to justice takes
him from Kansas City to the hell-hole of Salvation Creek. Will
he prevail in the final, bloody showdown?

Encounter at Salvation Creek

Paxton Johns

A Black Horse Western

ROBERT HALE · LONDON

© Paxton Johns 2011
First published in Great Britain 2011

ISBN 978-0-7090-9220-9

Robert Hale Limited
Clerkenwell House
Clerkenwell Green
London EC1R 0HT

www.halebooks.com

Typeset by
Derek Doyle & Associates, Shaw Heath
Printed and bound in Great Britain by
CPI Antony Rowe, Chippenham and Eastbourne

PART ONE

SALVATION CREEK

ONE

Born Gallant sat opposite William A. Pinkerton in the living room of his rented house, sipped some of his excellent single-malt Scotch whisky and listened intently to an intriguing tale.

William Pinkerton's father, Allan, had been an old friend of Gallant's late father. The two men had parted company in 1842 when Pinkerton set sail for America, first to manufacture barrels, then to become Chicago's first detective and eventually form his own detective agency. Twelve months before, in 1884, the Glaswegian founder of the agency that was already legendary had died in Chicago. Six months before, in England, Born's father, Noah Gallant, had died suddenly. Born had inherited the substantial Gallant estate in Surrey, had promptly handed the lot over to his brother and sister and set sail for the New World. There, called upon to fend for himself – though with a hefty bank balance to oil the wheels – it was only natural that he should look up the son of the man his father had so often talked about with affection, and respect.

William Pinkerton's rented house was on the outskirts of Kansas City. He had greeted Gallant warmly, and gone straight to the point.

'My office is in Chicago,' he said. 'I took over the western division last year when my father died, but because I'm a partner in the business with my brother, Robert, I like to make snap visits to regional offices. This month, one visit was forced on me: the man running our offices here in Kansas was murdered. Not wanting to rely on second-hand information, I came personally to investigate. On my second day here, I was shot from a distance by a man with a rifle; dumped from the saddle like a wet sack of coal.'

'Lucky to be alive,' Gallant commented gently, nodding at the other man's shoulder. 'I'd been wondering about the sling, the bandages.'

Pinkerton grunted. Continuing his tale without any further reference to his injuries, he said: 'I have come up with two possible reasons for that cowardly attack. The first is that someone cannot stand the sight of me, which would be no surprise at all: my family has put a lot of men behind prison bars; for them, revenge exacted on either one of us would be sweet. However, taking into account the previous brutal murder, it's possible someone is attempting to take over what is now a massive and highly profitable business: The Pinkerton National Detective Agency.'

'If that's the idea,' Gallant said, 'why start here in Kansas? Why not Chicago, or New York?'

'That's a point that had occurred to me, too. Hitting my man here doesn't seem to make sense. However, taking over Pinkertons also seems out of the question. The organization's tentacles are spread wide, and this is a massive country. Transport and communication are still so primitive, a coordinated attack on all the offices would be impossible. So I have come up with a third possibility: an investigation being carried out by the Pinkertons is getting too close to the truth. The murder, and the attempt on my life, are warnings.'

'Any particular investigation that hits you in the eye?'

'Nothing current.' Pinkerton sipped his whisky, then smiled grimly. 'Hence the fourth possibility.'

Gallant raised his eyebrows. 'Which is?'

'Someone, very soon, is going to approach us with the offer of a job. Could be an investigation, could be supplying security.' He waved a hand vaguely. 'Somebody doesn't want that to happen, and these shootings are warning us off in advance.'

'It would have to be a job of immense importance,' Gallant said, 'to warrant such drastic action.'

'Or something that means a lot to a particular person, or organization, but not a whole lot to anyone else. And that leaves me with a problem. Clearly, I have to find out what the hell is going on. My base is Chicago, so I'm not up to date with what's going on here in Kansas. Also, because I do not know who I can trust, I cannot hand responsibility for the investigation to anyone inside my own damn organization.'

'You need an outsider,' Gallant said.

'Preferably one who knows next to nothing about the Pinkertons, or life here in America. Someone to whom everything is new and therefore to be looked upon with suspicion.'

'An accurate description of yours truly,' Gallant said, grinning.

'The vacant position in the Kansas office had been filled when I arrived here. The second in command naturally moved into the top job. His name's Max Tremblay. I've left him in charge, but I don't trust him.'

'You think he was behind the shootings?'

'I don't know.'

'At which point another question springs to mind,' Gallant said. 'You're a partner in a big organization, offices across the United States, a lot of work done for the government including the foiling of a plot to assassinate Lincoln – so why not simply get rid of this fellow? If you admit you don't trust him, why leave him in charge in the first place?'

Pinkerton's eyes had narrowed. 'Because, like my late father, first and foremost I'm a detective. Putting Tremblay in temporary control may make him over confident: if he's involved in some kind of plot, I'm giving him the rope from which he can fashion the noose to hang himself. If, on the other hand, I get rid of him, I've learned nothing, and achieved little other than the removal of the present danger. That danger will almost certainly come back to haunt me unless I get to the root of the problem.'

'Or I do it for you.'

'I've got no choice in the matter. I must return to Chicago today, and here in Kansas City you are the only man I can trust.'

'Nobody else in the office?'

'Probably, but I'm not familiar with the staff, and in any case they'll all be controlled by Tremblay.'

'You want me to present myself to this fellow, and offer my services.'

'Exactly. If he had anything to do with the shootings, he'll want any investigation to fall flat. If there is some deadly game afoot, the killings are likely to continue.' He gazed with a critical eye at Gallant. 'We need to approach whoever is behind this from the side, lull them into a false sense of security. You, now, Gallant, I'm quite sure you can act the simpleton, if called upon so to do?'

'Born to it,' Gallant said, 'if you'll excuse the pun.'

'Then that will convince him he should hire you. He will expect you to take time bumbling your way through investigative procedures for which you have no talent, and eventually return to him shamefaced and empty-handed.'

'Then I'll be off,' Gallant said. 'Tally ho and all that rot.'

Pinkerton chuckled. Then he said, 'Before you

leave, I should warn you that there is one further possibility.'

'My life is in danger.'

'I can't rule it out. Tremblay might want to make damn sure your investigation bears no fruit, in which case I could be sending you to your death.

'Believe it or not,' Born Gallant said as he put down his glass, 'I'm actually a hard man to kill.'

The man sitting behind the desk was fat and slovenly, with eyes set too close to a fat blob of a nose. He was frowning. The stub of a cigar was smouldering beneath a thin moustache. He reached up, removed it from between wet lips with a finger and thumb. Ash sprinkled the stained front of his black suit. He brushed at it and glowered at the fair-haired man sitting in front of him.

'What the hell kind of a name,' he said, 'is Born Gallant?'

'Bit of a silly one, actually,' Gallant said, playing the upper class twerp to perfection. 'If there was a J after the B it might be understandable. Make me a Norwegian or something like that. Scandinavian at the very least – and, come to think of it, there was some mention of Viking blood in the old veins—'

'Next question,' Max Tremblay said, cutting in brusquely. 'What can a young Englishman with a damn silly name and the blood of Vikings in his veins do for me? What are you doing sitting in my office, Gallant?'

'Didn't your secretary tell you?'

12

'I think,' Tremblay said, 'she was rendered speech-less.'

Gallant grinned. 'I seem to have that effect on people I meet. Remarkable really, can't understand why. . . .'

He trailed off. Tremblay was gazing up at the ceiling, his lips a thin line.

'Sorry,' Gallant said meekly. 'I tend to do that: wander off at a tangent. The truth is I'm a private investigator and, as I heard rumours of a ticklish situation, I thought I'd wander in and offer my services.'

'To the man now in charge of the Pinkertons' Kansas office? An outpost of the world's most powerful detective agency?'

'Mm. Bit thick I suppose but, you know, nothing ventured – isn't that what they say? And the little bird that brought me the news did say the problem was thorny.'

'In the extreme,' Tremblay confirmed.

He sat back. His eyes, Gallant noticed, were now thoughtful; his fingers were laced across the fancy vest under his black jacket in a manner that suggested he was indeed chewing on a ticklish problem. The stub of cigar had been jettisoned, and was smouldering in an ashtray fashioned from the hoof of a buffalo. Acrid smoke curled. Remembering the role he was playing, Gallant allowed his nostrils to quiver sensitively. He flapped a hand in front of his face, and adopted an expression indicating extreme distaste.

'You say you're an investigator,' Tremblay said. 'Tell me, what's your success rate?'

'I'll be better placed to tell you when I've tackled your problem.'

'What does that mean?'

'Results on which to base statistics are a bit thin on the ground.'

'You're saying you've never done any investigating? I'm your first client?'

' 'Fraid so.'

Then the implication of the flat statement made by the superintendent of the Pinkerton National Detective Agency's central operations hit home, and Gallant beamed.

'Crikey,' he said. 'That sounds as if I've got the job.'

'The man who was in charge of the Pinkertons' operations here in Kansas was murdered: shot down as he rode home. And there's much worse,' Tremblay said. 'William Pinkerton, the brother of the man who created this business, came down from Chicago to investigate – and he, too, has been shot.'

'That is bad luck!'

'Luck?' Tremblay sneered. 'The only luck is the shot wasn't fatal.'

'And that luck could be considered good, or bad,' Gallant said, 'depending on your point of view.'

There was a heavy silence. Gallant could have bitten his tongue. For the first time since he'd entered the office, he'd said something that sounded halfway intelligent – and that was a mistake. He tried a silly grin. Tremblay's hard look didn't alter.

'Pinkerton's injured,' he said, expelling breath, 'but he'll be back. In his absence, and until he finds a suitable replacement for the dead man, I am in charge here. My priority is to discover who fired those shots. If I had my way I'd give the job to several of our most experienced agents. However,' he said, 'I've been overruled.'

'Enter yours truly,' Gallant said.

Tremblay nodded slowly, his lips pursed. That single inane utterance seemed to have convinced him: his whole expression registered satisfaction and approval.

'I may be making the biggest mistake of my life,' he said, 'but you're so damn unbelievable that the impossible becomes probable; I think you might pull it off, so I'm hiring you to bring to justice the man who murdered the head of our Kansas office and came close to doing exactly the same to William Pinkerton.'

'Isn't this the point where I pull out a notebook and start asking questions?'

'A waste of your time, and mine. I've put all the salient facts down in writing. There's a suspect. His name's Wilson Teager. He's wanted by the law in Texas, and Arizona Territory. They say he's an outlaw with a heart of stone who's killed four men in cold blood. I say he's a mean, cowardly cur who shoots men in the back and lies to build his reputation. A man of your calibre' – Tremblay looked Gallant straight in the eye – 'will handle the son of a bitch without raising a sweat.'

He leaned back, slid open a drawer, and flipped a sheet of paper on to the desk. 'Take that with you when you leave, Gallant. And don't bother coming back unless you've got the man who shot Pinkerton hog-tied over your saddle, or you're carrying his bloody scalp in your pale English hands.'

A remarkable transformation occurred by the time Born Gallant had left the Pinkerton's Main Street offices, ridden across town to the southern outskirts of Kansas City and shut behind him the door of his cheap hotel room. The foppish character had disappeared. Narrow rounded shoulders had mysteriously squared and broadened. A drooping five feet ten had become an erect six feet one inch. Floppy hair the colour of summer straw had been brushed back from the high forehead. Mild blue eyes that had looked out on the world with childlike wonderment now held a steely glint.

The room was musty. Four walls enclosed a bed, a table and a washstand with cracked water jug. As he dropped on to the table the paper given to him by Max Tremblay, Gallant was oblivious of the meanness of his surroundings, and was already planning his next move.

In the warm sunshine outside the Pinkertons' offices he had glanced at Tremblay's notes just long enough to find out where the suspected killer was likely to be found. It was his only lead, but it was likely to be a good one and the directions would lead him like an arrow into deadly danger.

If Max Tremblay was a traitor, he almost certainly wanted Gallant dead.

TWO

Some thirty miles south and west of Kansas City, a settlement crouched on a muddy creek that trickled lazily into the mighty Missouri. The village, built on bald slopes tumbling down to the yellow water, had been founded more than half a century ago by a starving traveller called Mo Tancred. Lips cracked, his tongue swollen with thirst, the tenderfoot from back East had for weeks been wandering blindly in the flat, windswept Kansas wilderness.

When Tancred finally brought his bony mule to an exhausted halt near the water, he had at first believed it to be another mirage. Then, thirst slaked and muscles slack with relief, he counted his blessings and began at once to build a dwelling from thick sods. While his muscles worked, cutting and lifting, fetching and carrying and stacking ever higher, his mind kept pace. The location, he decided, should be called Salvation Creek: he had reached it in the nick of time, so that was surely an apt name for the spot that had saved his bacon but which he knew instinc-

18

tively would also be his final resting place.

Somehow, the founder of Salvation Creek had acquired an Indian wife, the daughter of a Sioux brave. Eventually she had provided him with a son. That son was now in late middle-age. A dull but enterprising man, he had many years ago turned the tall timber house that had replaced his father's soddy – which happened to be within spitting distance of the creek – into a saloon. Despite being a 'breed in a land where they were despised, Sundown Tancred was also something of a humorist. In tune with his father's whimsy he had named his hostelry Last Chance and, according to the paper given to Born Gallant by Max Tremblay, Sundown Tancred's saloon was where the man he needed to talk to could be located.

Gallant's three-hour ride south-west from Kansas city had been uneventful, though several times he had experienced a familiar tingling at the nape of his neck that suggested strongly that he was being watched. Watched . . . or followed? Determined to put his suspicions to rest he had reined in his mount several times, as if resting, and casually surveyed his backtrail. He had seen nothing, heard nothing, and with a wry smile had watched the dust of his own passing drift away like gunsmoke on the evening breeze before pressing on towards Salvation Creek.

He rode in when the sun was a fiery red ball on the western horizon, the thin clouds across its face like ragged flames torn by the wind. Against this magnificent backdrop Salvation Creek was a disappointment, a crude cardboard cut-out on a stage of despair. Twenty years after Mo Tancred's death the settlement still consisted of no more than a score or so of unpainted timber dwellings clinging precariously to the slopes, with sagging galleries, and dark windows and doors like gaping, toothless mouths.

Gallant viewed the town with a critical eye. The rough dwellings, he noticed, had been erected haphazardly, the new alongside the old, without any thought given to town planning; the narrow, churned-up track wound its way between them like a rope tossed carelessly downhill by a man looking in another direction. Within that jumble of buildings a man was forced to ride blind. Gallant, knowing the saloon's location, simply headed downhill. As he allowed his horse to find its own way between the houses, oil lamps were already lighting grim rooms from which, Gallant knew, suspicious eyes were watching his progress.

When he emerged on the banks of a creek turned blood-red by the rays of the setting sun, he saw a hitch rail in front of a tottering building that might have emerged from the imagination of the American writer, Edgar Allen Poe.

At the rail, several ragged horses stood dozing.

Last Chance, Gallant mused, just about summed up the place.

It was at that point that Born Gallant mentally girded his loins. He was unarmed but for his agile brain and lightning fast reactions. And Salvation Creek was not just the most depressing town he'd ever seen, it was also well known as a safe haven used by some of the West's most wicked and violent outlaws.

Visitors to Last Chance entered by sweeping aside a hanging blanket that had probably been snatched from the lathered back of Mo Tancred's long-dead mule and left unwashed. The greasy material brushed across Born Gallant's face. The filth of many decades desecrated his lips and invaded his nostrils. Then the big windowless room assaulted him with its stench of animals, humans, alcohol and tobacco smoke – all as ripe and rich as last month's meat left out in the sun.

He rocked back on his heels. Every man in that room became as still as death. Gallant thought, for one terrible moment, that he had been stricken with deafness; a sudden, eerie silence had settled over the room's occupants. Feeling like the condemned man with his foot on the first step up to the gallows, Born Gallant moved to one side, stood back against the wall and took stock.

The room was not large, and the stifling atmosphere made it feel even smaller. The board ceiling was the floor of the room above, and seemed about to collapse. The saloon's floor was packed dirt, strewn with sawdust filthy enough to have been gathered from logs used to construct the building – what, forty years ago? A plank bar stretched the length of the back wall. It rested on empty barrels, some with sprung staves. The bar sagged in places under its load of stained bottles and glasses, earthenware jugs that undoubtedly contained the kind of spirits that would render a steer unconscious, several rifles and what looked like a shotgun. Spittoons were empty; the floor's sawdust was dotted with wet blobs.

About the rest of that cramped room a few tables were scattered. Unshaven, ill-clad men sat at two of them. They had been playing cards. Gallant's unexpected entrance had sent hands drifting towards pistols and knives, and eyes that were as expressive as wet stones had turned in his direction.

At the end of the bar, two men were standing. Both were tall and rangy. Their garb was black, the weapons they carried worn with an ease and panache that suggested familiarity and frequent use. Both of those men had given Gallant but a fleeting glance. Now their backs were turned and they were deep in conversation.

Telling himself that those two, of all the riff raff gathered in the room, were the ones to watch, Gallant heard a voice at his elbow say, 'If you're after a glass of milk, son, Millie's dairy's the top end of town.'

Gallant grinned. 'Glory be,' he said softly, 'I've entered a room inhabited by uncivilized boors, and the first man I encounter is a gent. Tell me, kind sir, you don't happen to know if Wilson Teager's quaffing ale in here, do you?'

The response was a blank look; the man stepped back, as if in shock, either from Gallant's strange way of talking or the name he had dropped. With a shake

22

of the head Gallant clapped the gaunt and suddenly fearful fellow on his shoulder, watched him sidle away through the curtained doorway, and set off for the bar.

Deliberately, but without trying too hard, Gallant was able to put into his demeanour that certain something that told the armed men in the room that he posed no threat. He made his way slowly across the filthy floor without a hint of swagger in his walk. They relaxed, and turned back to their cards and their drinks.

The huge man behind the bar was watching the newcomer impassively. Another to be wary of? Gallant wondered, as he neared the bar and picked up the man's ripe scent.

The 'breed was fully six-foot-six tall, and broad enough to make that height seem average. His hair was a dull black, with a centre parting exposing a scalp last washed when he was a papoose. A thick plait hung in front of each massive shoulder, their ends tied with knotted rags. Most of the man's body was hidden behind a grubby apron that would have covered a Brahma bull. Atop the bar, close to one of his huge hands, there rested a pick helve worn shiny with use.

Gallant slowed as he approached that crude bar, for now his mind was busy deciding on tactics. It was the merest, token mental effort, for he knew full well that the character he had honed over the years dictated his actions without the need for thought. So it was that when he put two hands on the rough planks,

23

leaned forward conspiratorially and winked at the massive barman, he knew full well that the words that issued from his lips were just as likely to get him killed as break the ice.

'I thought I'd been landed with an impossibly silly name,' he said just loud enough for the words to carry to the nearest tables, 'but when I heard yours I thought, now there's a name that really takes the biscuit.'

He straightened up, and grinned.

'I do have the pleasure of talking to Sundown Tancred, don't I? My name's Born Gallant, and I'm here looking for outlaws – well, one outlaw in particular, actually.'

And with that, he thrust out his hand.

As he did so, his left hand contrived to knock the shiny pick helve to the floor. It fell with a clatter dulled by the sawdust. Looking abashed, Gallant bent, picked it up, and leant it against the bar – on his side.

Again he thrust out his hand.

There was a moment's hesitation. Then the big 'breed clasped it in his, and squeezed with the lightest of grips. There was grease on his palm, grease on his thick fingers, grease causing the thin film of perspiration at his hairline to glisten. His eyes were like black buttons set in buffalo fat turned yellow with age.

He released Gallant's hand, let his arm drop so that it twitched his dirty apron to one side to reveal the plaited leather sap tucked in his belt.

He said, 'What'll it be?'

'Well,' Gallant said, 'milk was suggested, but I think I'll have a shot glass of your finest whiskey, and hang the expense.'

The 'breed splashed whiskey from an unlabelled bottle into a glass so smeared that when he'd finished pouring it could have been full, or empty. He lifted it high, wiped it with a forefinger, his little finger delicately cocked, and handed it to Gallant.

Gallant, noting the contempt, tossed back the whiskey with a flick of the wrist.

He put the empty glass down.

He said, 'I'm looking for a man called Wilson Teager.'

'Don't turn around too sudden,' said Sundown Tancred, 'or you'll knock him off his feet.'

The men from the end of the bar had moved closer on boots as silent as moccasins. When Gallant turned he saw that both of them were behind him, crowding close, but just far enough apart for a turn of the head to be needed to appraise each man in turn.

Canny, he thought. Wise to the way battles are won or lost.

Their height, Gallant saw, was all they had in common. The man on the left was a gunslinger pure and simple, untidy, unshaven, his eyes as dull and cold as used nickels but the two six-guns in holsters with rawhide ties shiny from frequent use. The lean man on the right appeared taller because he held himself erect. A gunslinger, too, but of a superior

25

type, Gallant judged. His flashing black eyes were hard, intelligent, and knowing. Thin lips were almost hidden by a full black beard flecked with grey, and were twisted slightly in what could have been a sneer, or wry amusement.

Christ, Gallant thought, *this fellow thinks he knows what I'm going to say. All right, we'll see about that. Let's see if we can shock some of that smugness out of him.*

'Wilson Teager?'

The man nodded.

'I've been told you had a hand in one murder, and in the shooting of William Pinkerton. Pulled the trigger on both occasions, actually.'

For the second time in the space of ten minutes, the Last Chance went eerily quiet. But this time it was different. Heads remained bent, but the silence was not absolute. Though all conversation had ceased, the continuing snap of playing card against playing card was like the irregular ticking of a clock counting down the seconds to sudden death.

'You walk in here naked,' Wilson Teager said huskily, 'and have the gall to say that to me?'

'Well, not exactly naked—'

'Where's your gun?'

'Wouldn't know what to do with it. Never had one, never held one – at least, not one like that.'

Gallant gestured, palm-up, to the the bone-handled six-gun hanging low on Teager's right thigh. He was looking at the gun's twin on the man's other thigh when there was a blur of movement, too fast for his eye to follow, and suddenly the man's six-gun was resting in Gallant's outstretched hand.

The man in black let his hand fall away.

'Golly,' Gallant said, genuinely impressed by the speed of the draw.

'So now you're holding one,' Teager said. 'You've got a gun, and you've got your chance. It could be your last – so what are you going to do?'

Carefully, thoughtfully, Gallant turned the weapon in his hand.

Between the two men who were now waiting for his response he had a clear view of the tables. The four men playing poker at the nearest table, though all too aware that they were in the line of fire, were determined to appear engrossed in their game. The man with his back to Gallant was holding a fan of greasy cards, and deliberating. The two men on his left and right were waiting with their eyes lowered, their hands fiddling with the gold coins that lay in heaps before them: Gallant saw the glitter of five dollar half-eagles, ten dollar eagles. The man opposite the character labouring over his discards was leaning back in his chair studying the glass of whiskey he held in his hand.

Something extra special's required here, Gallant thought, his eyes pensive as he examined the six-gun. It was, he saw, a Colt Peacemaker. He knew the make but, no, he had spoken the truth because this particular model Colt was one he had never held in his hands.

But a pistol's a pistol when all's said and done he thought, remembering the wonderful old duelling

27

pistols by London gunsmiths Wogdon & Barton and Purdey he had held and admired. Suppressing a grin as the thrill of approaching action coursed through his veins, he lifted the Peacemaker level with his chest. He held it clumsily, as if examining it, the butt between the fingers of his right hand. The barrel was pointing vaguely to the left. As if by accident, his thumb was curled around the trigger.

'Single action?' he said, looking at Teager.

The gunman nodded, noting with obvious scorn Gallant's awkward grip.

'So to fire it,' Gallant said, 'I have to pull back this thingamajig, then yank on this bit down here,' Gallant said.

His forefinger was curled awkwardly over the hammer. As he snapped the weapon to full cock, he sensed the two men recoiling, looked up wide-eyed and innocent at two gunslingers leaping out of the line of fire, hands dropping to their guns.

Gallant's thumb squeezed the trigger.

There was a deafening crack, a spurt of flame from the Peacemaker's muzzle followed by the tinkle of breaking glass. Then a silence in which eardrums rang and into which someone uttered a soft, disbelieving, 'Jesus holy H Christ!'

The poker player with his back to the bar was gazing in astonishment at the cards he held in his hand. He was still holding the open fan of five cards. The fully exposed card on the right of the fan was the ace of spades. A neat hole had been punched in the black spade at the card's centre. Across the table, the poker player who had been morosely staring into his whiskey was left holding nothing but splinters. The glass had shattered in his hand, leaving it wet with strong spirit and tendrils of blood.

The tableau held for a long ten seconds. The four poker players were frozen in shock. Teager and his companion were crouched ten feet away on either side of Gallant, each with one hand on the bar, each holding a levelled six-gun.

Sundown Tancred broke the spell. He coughed, spat, and spoke with a sneer in his guttural voice as he turned away in disgust.

'The man held that shooter upside down, used his thumb on the trigger,' he said. 'Any way you look at it, that must be the luckiest damn shot ever fired.'

'You're absolutely right,' Gallant said.

He turned towards the big saloonist, seemed to bump carelessly against the bar, and once again flame belched from the Peacemaker's muzzle. The plaited leather sap was plucked from Tancred's belt. It flew high, and knocked a bottle from the shelf. Again glass smashed. The reek of strong liquor rose to sting the nostrils, bring water to the eyes.

'There's all kinds of luck,' Gallant said, philosophically, 'and what my daddy always told me was that a man makes his own.' He cocked his head to look hard at Wilson Teager, who had straightened to his full height. 'He told me lots more, of course – but you'll hear more of that later, and most will be hard for you to swallow. What I'd like to know *now* is if I'm right; if you, Teager, were involved in those shootings?'

'If I was,' Teager said, 'would I be likely to tell you?'

'It might be advisable,' Gallant said. 'One man's luck is often another man's misfortune – something you should bear in mind when considering your answer.'

'You talk tough, shoot fancy, but you're a man on his own with the odds stacked against him. You kill one of us, the other will get you for sure.'

Gallant grinned. 'That will be your unpleasant partner, because I'll make damn sure you're the first to go, old boy.'

'Old boy,' Teager echoed softly, and there was a sudden ugly glint in his eyes. He pursed his lips, then took a deep breath and flipped his pistol into the holster on his left thigh. His partner followed suit.

'Why would I gun down Pinkerton?'

'My guess would be for money; someone's paying you to point the gun, pull the trigger. As to why he's wasting good money, that's something the man who's now heading the Pinkertons has been puzzling over. He suspects all kinds of devilish plots, perhaps leading all the way up to the United States president. That makes me wonder why I'm talking to you. I hate to ruin your day, shatter your confidence and all that, but from where I'm standing I'd say you haven't got enough brains to order yourself a drink.'

There was a harsh rasp as somewhere in the room a man nervously scraped a match and fired up a cigarette. Gallant's words seemed to have hit Teager between the eyes and taken away his power of speech. *Definitely not used to being spoken to in that way,* Gallant thought; *he's been knocked off balance, doesn't know what I'm going to do next. But that won't last. His mind's gone blank, he's gazing into the unknown, but he'll recover fast and rage will take over and then. . . .*

'Something else my daddy told me,' Gallant said casually, 'was to watch a man's eyes and act on what's revealed. That's always seemed like sound advice, but I told you earlier it was something you'd find hard to swallow. So, though it will be of little comfort, I'm apologizing in advance.'

With that he took a fast step sideways, and with a short swing carrying the full weight of his shoulder behind it he slammed the big Peacemaker backhand across Teager's bearded jaw.

There was a crack as of bone shattering. The big man's head rocked sideways. His mouth gaped red revealing splintered teeth. For a moment he stood motionless. Then his legs buckled and he went down hard. He hit the dirt floor with the back of his head. His eyes rolled. Flat on his back he lay there, one hand twitching, breathing wetly.

Gallant caught a flash of movement to his left. Like lightning, he swung the Peacemaker to bear on Teager's companion. The man's hand had flashed to his six-gun. His teeth were bared, his eyes blazing. Gallant grinned, waggled the Peacemaker's barrel, watched the gunman's hand fall away.

For several seconds, Wilson Teager lay still. Then he blinked, shook his head and groaned in agony. He rolled on to his side, then on to his front. He lifted his upper body off the floor on quivering arms. Head hanging, he struggled to rise.

'My good man,' Gallant said cheerfully, 'please don't bother to get up on my account.'

Leaning back, taking all his weight on his left foot, he kicked Teager in the face. The tall man jerked spasmodically, flopped, then lay still.

Gallant tucked the Peacemaker in his waistband and slipped unhurriedly out through the greasy curtain. Behind him there was a leaden silence, but even as he walked towards his horse there erupted a muffled babble of incoherence that assaulted his ears and caused him to wince. He wondered, briefly, if he had gone too far.

His intention when he rode into Salvation had been to poke a metaphorical stick into the hornets' nest he had been directed to by Max Tremblay for, the truth was, he was a newcomer in a strange land and feeling his way without the benefit of a white cane. So why struggle to hunt down powerful and ruthless men, he had reasoned, when moving in hard and fast on the killer they employed would give them food for thought and possibly sting them into actions that might leave them exposed.

Viciously attacking Wilson Teager had made a point that no man present in that saloon would ever forget, and one certainty was that from that dingy room in the Last Chance saloon his reputation would spread like a rampaging prairie fire.

First part of the job done, then, Gallant thought –

but to enable him to move to the next stage he now had to get clear of the village that climbed like a precarious stack of mouldering timber from the banks of the muddy creek.

Hesitating for a moment, he listened to the swirl of noise from the Last Chance. It could only be a few short seconds, he knew, before the blanket was brushed aside and armed men poured into the street baying for his blood. Hurrying now, he took out his silver-trimmed pocket knife, snicked open the blade and ran to the horses tied at the rail. The knife's blade was razor-sharp. There were five horses, all standing hip-shot, all still dozing. Gallant sliced five times; five times greasy leather parted and a cinch fell into two separate, useless parts. Then he snapped the knife shut and ran for his horse.

As he swung into the saddle and turned his mount towards the steep, narrow street, he knew he had made his mark with a vengeance. If Teager and his companion were the bushwhackers who had killed a Pinkerton agent and injured the organization's chief, they'd now go crawling back to their masters. News of his violent arrival on the scene would be treated seriously. The questions he had asked Teager would convince them that he, Gallant could seriously endanger their plans, and steps would be taken to remove the enigmatic Englishman who had made two hardened gunslingers look like a couple of schoolgirls.

From now on he'd be a hunted man, and that was the best he could hope for from the evening's work.

As he urged his mount up the steep, muddy street, the noise behind him suddenly swelled. Reluctantly, Gallant raked with his spurs. The horse responded. Instinctively picking the easiest path, it climbed that slippery hillside with the nimble bounds of a mountain goat.

Then a shot cracked in the night. Gallant tensed, flattened himself along the straining horse's neck. A second shot rang out, a third – and still, unaccountably, there was no whisper of hot lead, no vicious plucking at Gallant's clothes as expected bullets hummed perilously close.

Can they be that bad? Gallant thought wildly. *Are their senses addled by drink, is their eyesight blurred, are their pistols so old as to be of no use? What the hell is going on?*

Suddenly there was a crackling volley of shots, and now hot lead was flying dangerously close. Shutters banged as, on either side of him, villagers in their houses hastily took cover and secured their dwellings. The light that had been seeping across the dust and the mud blinked out, and nothing was left to guide him but the pale light of the rising moon.

Then, unbelievably, a horse drew level with him, and out of the gloom a voice sang joyfully.

'I've done my best,' it cried, 'I've held them back as best I could to give you time to get clear. But that best hasn't stopped them so now you must ride like the wind or all my good work comes to nothing – and that's something I won't stand for.'

And with that a young woman with dark hair richly flowing in the wind spurred her mount close enough to Born Gallant's for him to feel the brush of her thigh as she rode by and with every stride of her sleek pony the gap between them began to lengthen.

THREE

It took them a matter of minutes to put the settlement of Salvation Creek behind them. As they crested the rise that took them away from the creek and the jumble of shabby houses clinging to the side of the hill and set off at a gallop across the flat, Kansas prairie, Gallant found himself falling further and further behind the amazing young woman. Determination clamped his jaw and narrowed his eyes as he settled to the chase; bewilderment at her sudden appearance and astonishment at the boldness and undoubted accuracy of her shooting caused his mind to whirl.

He rode north through a land of haunting beauty. Pale moonlight stripped the world of colour. Trees at the edge of Gallant's vision were muted pastel greys rimmed with light, and under limitless skies the soft breeze turned mile upon mile of rippling grass into the moving surface of an endless ocean.

Gallant's rescuer's reckless, headlong flight across that eerie prairie had the effect of drawing them rapidly away from tenacious pursuers whose mounts must have been tethered at the side of the Last Chance. One or two shots rang out, the detonations as faint and ineffective as those of distant firecrackers. By the light of the pale moon, as he risked one glance over his shoulder, Gallant saw that there were but two riders, and it was clear that they had now given up the chase: they had reined in and were already swinging their mounts back towards Salvation Creek.

A relieved smile tugged at his lips. He knew that he and the young woman had got away by the skin of their teeth, and that the pursuit had fallen away just in time. No horse that lived could keep up such a furious gallop indefinitely, and even as that thought crossed Gallant's mind he sensed the young woman's frantic pace slackening. He found himself first closing, then drawing level with the sleek pony that was now lathered and clearly labouring.

'Enough,' Gallant said, reaching out to touch the young woman's shoulder. 'Pull in to those trees, we're done with running so let's rest for a while. No sense in killing two fine animals when there's nothing of any danger to us within a hundred square miles.'

Dark eyes flashed his way. 'Do you always talk and act in extremes?'

'Invariably,' Gallant said, grinning. 'Got it from my daddy. Get in the first blows, in tight situations talk the hind leg off a donkey to confuse but make sure there's at least a grain of truth tucked away in the verbosity.'

'Nevertheless, this time you came close to losing your life,' she said, shaking her head. 'Wilson Teager is a dangerous man; still is, despite the damage you inflicted – probably even more so, because now he has a terrible score to settle. I'd say whoever sent you out here tonight has a lot to answer for.'

'As for me,' Gallant said, following her into the stand of trees and slipping easily from the saddle, 'I'd like to shake the hand of whoever sent you to Salvation Creek, because it's pretty clear you saved my bacon.'

He was drawing his water canteen from a saddle-bag as he spoke. Without bothering to look, he tossed it in the young woman's direction. She caught it with one hand. When she drank deeply of the cool water, her eyes were watching him. He stood with hands on hips.

'We'd best slacken the cinches,' he said, 'let the horses graze, rest a while.'

'Don't get cocksure; those men could be regrouping, so forget all thoughts of a lengthy rest. Besides, we can't let the horses stand too long. In the night air they'll cool down quickly.'

'So will I. Things got extraordinarily heated back there in the Last Chance. And now I'm wondering what you were doing in that tumbledown settlement, and how much you saw of that fracas in the saloon.'

'All of it, from your impudent approach to that big bear Sundown Tancred, to the final kick that removed most of Teager's remaining teeth. A kind man let me slip in through that filthy curtain. I was carrying my rifle, with a full magazine. I was about to use it to take control of the proceedings when you went off like an unstable stick of dynamite.'

Gallant chuckled. 'Unstable's my middle name. The ones on either side of it are Born, and Gallant.'

'I'm Melody Lake,' she said. 'My daddy decided those two sounded purty enough without squeezing in a third.'

'Well, Melody, you still haven't told me what you were doing in Salvation Creek.'

He caught the canteen as she threw it back to him, wiped the neck with his palm and drained it in one draught. She was watching him when he again turned from fastening his saddle-bag. In the moon-light her eyes were twinkling.

'Well?'

'Saving you. That's what I was doing.' She smiled quizzically. 'Tell me, Born Gallant, were those shots you fired in there lucky?'

'They were made with a heavy Peacemaker Colt I'd never fired, held the way a cow might hold a rifle which is no way at all, and I don't recall bothering to take aim. It was tricky sharpshooting done for show, done to impress, and that was achieved. But lucky? No I don't think so – I think those shots were mirac-ulous.'

'You're English, aren't you?'

'To the true blue core.'

'Which explains your false modesty. I think you knew exactly where those slugs would go, but that doesn't explain why you were taking such a big risk;

why you went up against that blackguard, Wilson Teager, and his mad dog of a sidekick.'

'My answer to that is to be evasive, but to add that I don't believe in coincidence. There's no doubt in my mind we were both in Salvation Creek looking for Teager, though perhaps for different reasons. But I'll go a step further: different reasons, maybe, but reasons that in some way I haven't yet worked out must be closely connected.'

'What that means, if you think about it,' Melody Lake said softly, 'is that even without either of us answering a question, we're at least halfway to knowing why the other was keen to talk to that outlaw.'

'Bit like playing stud poker, actually,' Gallant said, suddenly serious, 'where the only two players left in the game are flatly refusing to turn over their hole card.'

FOUR

She came to him some time after midnight, creeping out of the deep shadows behind his rocking chair as he sat on the gallery in the moonlight. Boards creaked under her bare feet. The chair swayed a little as she rested her hands on his shoulders, her fingers gently kneading the muscles.

'What are you doing out here, old man?' she said softly, bending so that her breath warm was against his ear.

'Old man,' he mocked, and he turned to smile at her, a sturdy woman wearing a worn cloak over her flannel nightgown, her white hair pinned up, the fine lines engraved on her face over the years softened now by the flattering light. 'I'm waiting for my granddaughter, that's what I'm doing. She told me earlier she would ride back this way. Whatever it is she's doing would take time, she said, and as she'll almost certainly stay here for the rest of the night. . . .'

He shrugged, turning again to gaze without seeing

again into the moonlit distance, knowing he had left too much unsaid and uneasily awaiting the inevitable. She was his wife. He couldn't lie to her, but the alternative was to remain silent and he knew even that would not be tolerated.

Her hands slipped from his shoulders. She came around the chair, stood with her arms folded and her back to the rail and the luminous skies as she looked at him intently.

'What can possibly keep Melody out so late?'

'Things that are her business, not ours.'

'Hers – and yours; I've seen you both with your heads together, talking, I know you're sharing secrets. If what's happening is being done with your connivance, then you're not only old, you're a fool. She's a vulnerable young woman—'

'A *remarkable* young woman—'

'Taking absurd risks. I know she's tough as old boots, full of salt, but there are wicked men out there could snap her in half. What's she up to, Frank?'

'Ask her, not me. I can't lie to you, but I'm not going to betray a confidence.' He hesitated, biting his lip. 'All I can tell you is that she is . . . doing what she's doing to help someone, and because it's being done without their knowledge—'

'That someone wouldn't be her father, would it?' Sarah Lake said drily.

'Ask her,' Frank Lake repeated doggedly. 'Don't put me in a bad position, Sarah.'

'Whoa, now, don't you go blaming me. You got yourself into this fix, and as far as I can recall it's the first time in more than forty years that you've shut me out.'

'That's unfair, and it certainly wasn't the intention. Melody came to me. She asked my advice, told me what was discussed between us must go no further. She said something about powerful men, *dangerous* men, men who'll stop at nothing.'

'I see. First you blame me, then you blame her, now you're throwing in an element of risk so I'll keep my mouth tight shut.'

'Dammit, Sarah, I can't take any more of this—'

'*Is* she doing it for her daddy? Has our son got himself into something he can't handle? Does he need his *daughter* to get him out of a fix?'

'James started out as a lawyer, but always remember he's now a cattleman,' Lake said.

She stared. 'Is that a hint? Should I read something from that?'

'Go make us a hot drink,' he said wearily. 'And do some thinking while you're at it. You're an intelligent woman, Sarah. Most of the time you don't need me to spell things out for you.'

Sarah Lake took her time over brewing the coffee. If one fact had emerged from that short but acrimonious conversation it had come in Frank's last comment: most of the time she *could* work things out for herself – so why didn't she do that instead of badgering a tired old man?

She smiled fondly.

The kitchen was warm. She sat in her favourite

chair, the cloak pulled about her. The coffee pot bubbled hypnotically. The big clock ticked, its beat matching the whisper of her pulse. It would have been easy to doze – but however comfortable she was, there were pressing problems to be solved.

It was now ten years since she and Frank had moved into the small house on the very edge of the Rocking L ranch they'd founded. They'd done so because it had been quite clear it was time for their son, James, to take over the day-to-day running of Rocking L.

At that time he'd already been married for ten years to Rebecca, a young woman from Kansas City; their daughter Melody had been nine, and attending the local school. The arrangement had worked well: Sarah and Frank had settled easily into a comfortable retirement; James's hard work and Frank's long experience with the business side of ranching had seen Rocking L continue to prosper.

The picture was rosy, Sarah mused. And yet. . . .

Well, money troubles were out. James and Rebecca were happy together. Melody was training to be a lawyer. On the face of it there didn't appear to be a cloud on the horizon – so what in Hades was going on?

The uncharacteristic crudity of her thoughts made Sarah smile again, but the smile quickly faded.

Melody was now nineteen. Frank maybe didn't know it, but Sarah had watched her ride out that evening on her buckskin mare and had taken note of the Winchester rifle tucked into the saddle boot. It was now – she glanced at the big clock – almost two in the morning. So what should she, Sarah, make of it?

'James is a cattleman,' Frank had said. A throw-away remark? Or was there some meaning hidden in there? Likely there was because, despite his obvious unease, Frank was not the kind of man to say anything just to keep his lips flapping.

James was a cattleman but, more importantly, he was prosperous. So rather than looking for a way to dig himself out of a hole, he could be looking at new ways to increase Rocking L's prosperity. However, as far as Sarah was aware, the land they had was fully stocked, and no adjoining acreage was up for sale. With no space for more cattle, another possibility was for James to bring in pedigree bulls to increase the value of their herds – but Frank had made sure from the outset that he bought only prime stock.

Sarah eased herself stiffly out of the chair. The warm room was filled with the rich aroma of coffee. She took two cups from hooks, and as she filled them from the pot and added cream, she asked herself what could be left?

Well, she'd been scathing when Frank had mentioned danger, but if he'd got that from Melody there must be some truth in it. Dangerous men, he'd said. Men who'd stop at nothing. All right, but if Rocking L was in some kind of danger from ruthless men, the last thing you'd do would be to send your daughter out to confront them. Or your grand-daughter for that matter because, according to

Frank, James had been kept in the dark.

What you *would* do, Sarah mused, would be to talk to other ranchers and, if the danger was not confined to Rocking L, band together for mutual protection.

And as she stood there, the cups of coffee forgotten in her hands, Sarah Lake found herself recalling 1883, and what a bunch of wise ranchers had done down in the Cherokee Strip.

'Two days,' James Lake said. 'Might as well be two lifetimes. Without the Pinkertons, I can't see us getting the deal through in that time – if ever.'

He was sitting at his desk in the room set aside for an office in the Rocking L ranch house. His dark hair was tousled from continually running his fingers through it. Papers littered the desk. The fancy oil lamp with a bottle-green shade revealed a faint sheen of perspiration on Lake's face, and left a circle of dark shadows around the edges of the room.

Rebecca Lake was sitting in an easy chair just outside the circle of light, wrapped in a dressing gown; unable to sleep, she had just come downstairs. Strain showed on her face. It was bad enough her husband worrying himself sick, but here it was a couple of hours after midnight, her daughter was still out and she had no idea where she had gone.

James Lake saw her expression, and shrugged helplessly.

'She said nothing to me. I know she's been talking to Dad lately, but I can't imagine what they're up to.'

'Her being out may have nothing to do with your father.' Rebecca looked at her thumbnail, then shot a glance at James. 'Does your father know about Consolidated?'

'No. How can he? It doesn't exist.'

'He still plays an important part in the running of the ranch. Don't you think you should have told him?'

'No!'

Lake spoke loudly, then spun his swivel chair to face his wife. He saw he'd startled her, and his face softened. 'Maybe if we could have got the Pinkertons on our side, got some protection. But when that fell through—'

'Why did it? There's a consortium, the fees wouldn't have been a problem, so what happened?'

'When the gent running the Pinkertons' Kansas office was shot dead, a shifty looking character by the name of Tremblay moved up a rung. He gave me five minutes, half-listened to what I had to say then sent me packing.'

'And then William Pinkerton was shot,' Rebecca said softly, 'when this man you call shifty knew you might have been considering going over his head and all the way to the top. Doesn't that tell you something?'

'Of course it does.'

'You mean you believe he's lording over the Pinkertons' Kansas office, but taking bribes from those opposed to Consolidated? And those men are ruthless enough to murder people you and the other businessmen on your side would go to for help?'

'Or get others to do the job for them.' Lake shrugged. 'If we're to pull this off we've got to hope for the best, but expect the worst.'

'That's not an answer. All right, either you're being pessimistic, or there's something you're not telling me. Do you know for a fact the men opposed to Consolidated are behind those shootings?'

'No I don't. But I'm realistic: I don't believe in coincidence. I believe violent men from Texas stepped in to delay the Pinkertons' involvement in this business. Delayed: Pinkertons is too big an organization to stop for long, but those men have bought themselves time. Time to kill again – and from tomorrow we'll have two important businessmen here, in this house, enjoying our hospitality.'

'Would you mind fixing that front door before they get here. The catch has been broken for a month. How it stays shut truly baffles me.'

FIVE

The direction they rode was south from Salvation Creek, the pace moderate for there was no special need for haste and Wilson Teager was groggy, and in pain. His partner, the gunslinger whose name was Tyne Messner, kept a careful eye on him. Not only was Teager injured, the sheer unexpectedness and ferocity of what had befallen him in Sundown Tancred's saloon had left him burning with rage.

Mumbling raggedly and mostly incoherently through his injured mouth, he turned aside frequently to spit out tooth chippings as blood dribbled into his beard and dripped on his shirt front. He was fuming at the way he had handed the unknown Englishman called Born Gallant one of his Peacemakers. Couldn't believe he'd stood there like something carved from a block of wood as Gallant had drawn their attention with a show of crazy shooting then used the same six-gun to cold cock Teager.

Then, when Teager had climbed up off the floor and staggered outside, they'd discovered their horses' cinches had been slashed, and the men who mounted the pursuit had been held back by a slip of girl who'd sent slugs from a Winchester whistling by their ears as she used her knees to urge her buckskin pony up the steep hill.

The men of Last Chance who had accepted Teager's offer of a silver dollar each to ride after her and the Englishman had returned disconsolate, and with a measure of disbelief: they had been on fast, sure-footed horses familiar with the country, yet they had been outdistanced, left for dead.

Teager's silver dollars remained in his vest pocket. They left Salvation Creek knowing that they had been outsmarted.

They rode for the first ten miles with no sound to be heard but the steady drum of their horses' hoofs and the drone of Teager's monotonous swearing. The moon's light dimmed as thin high cloud spread across the night skies. The trail arrowed straight and true across flat, rippling grassland. Scattered stands of trees were undisturbed by the gentle, whispering wind, and it was into one such stand that the riders pulled to give their mounts a breather.

'Who the hell was that clown?' Teager growled wetly, as he slid from the saddle. 'What did he want, and how did he find us?'

'Tremblay must've told him.'

'Nuts to that. Tremblay's got that office sealed. For the next two days nothing goes in, nothing comes out.'

'Maybe, but he had you bang to rights. One

killing. Pinkerton badly wounded. Somehow he knows those bushwhackings were your handiwork.'

'He was guessing.'

'Or he got it from the horse's mouth.'

Messner was still in the saddle. His hands were folded on the horn. He watched Teager mulling over what he'd said.

'Tremblay again?' Teager ventured at last. 'You saying he's a treacherous skunk, he sold us out to that clown?'

'That, or he had good reason for pointing him in our direction.'

'What possible reason?'

'The obvious one,' Messner said, after a moment's thought. 'For some reason he had Gallant down as trouble. Tremblay figured if he sent him after us, you or me would gun him down, finish his game.'

Teager's laugh was ugly. 'Oh, he got the timing wrong, but he was right nonetheless: the next time I see Born Gallant, he's a dead man.'

After their remarkable escape from Salvation Creek and the subsequent deserved dalliance in the trees, Gallant and Melody Lake talked idly about this and that for almost a quarter hour. While their horses grazed, regained strength and the lightness returned to their step, Gallant, using bland words, tried cunningly to pry information from Melody. He got nothing for his trouble.

She's as tight as a clam with her information, he thought. Pretty, but a clam nonetheless – a clam deeply involved in troubles that the Pinkertons had been warned to stay out of, and that those stirring 'em up saw as important enough to hire men the likes of Wilson Teager.

Eventually they parted, and Gallant rode away knowing only that Melody Lake appeared to be pointing her sprightly pony's head north towards Kansas City. But was her destination before, after, or actually somewhere in the city? He didn't know, and didn't bother guessing.

His own destination was the settlement from which he and Melody had only recently escaped; he figured he'd been awake so long he might as well retrace his steps and make a night of it. He'd learnt nothing from Melody Lake, didn't know who she was or how she was involved. Teager and his companion were in the thick of things, so seeing if he could learn something useful from the two outlaws seemed like a good idea. But were they using that festering hole on the banks of the muddy creek as a base, or were they there because the Last Chance was their nearest watering hole?

A hunch said Salvation Creek was where they were unrolling their blankets, but the man with money who was paying for their guns would surely want more salubrious surroundings. Teager would be in an ugly mood. He'd want to know why he hadn't been warned about Gallant. The way to find out would be to talk to his boss – and he'd be in a hurry. With that thought spurring him on, Gallant drove his tired horse hard back towards Salvation Creek, hoping to sneak back down the street twisting between run-down shacks in time to pick up the outlaws' trail.

He succeeded, by the skin of his teeth. He eased his nervous mount with caution down that rutted track to find the curtain pulled across Last Chance's door, the single window aglow, but no sign of life. Then, above the muted gurgle of muddy water and a smothered oath followed by the sound of glass breaking from Tancred's saloon, he caught the fading rattle of hoofs. Seconds later he was through the town and continuing in a southerly direction, following two riders that instinct told him were Teager and his partner.

And if it's not them, Gallant thought philosophically, then I'm out for a pleasant ride in the moonlight.

For the first hour he stayed well back, riding off trail, trying as best he could to keep sparse stands of trees between him and the outlaws. After some ten miles or so, they also pulled off the trail. Gallant waited. The sound of their voices carried clearly on the night air. He thought he recognized Teager's distinctive tones, the heat of his anger, and was reassured: at least he wasn't following a couple of drunken ranchers heading home to their wives.

After that brief rest another ten miles was covered before the terrain roughened, thicker woodland encroached on the trail and Gallant was forced to draw much closer to the two outlaws. The track wound through dark trees whose branches trailed.

The scent of pine mingled with dust. Needles deadened the sound of hoofs. Suddenly Gallant was near enough to the two men to hear fragments of conversation. A name was mentioned – he was sure of that – but too indistinctly for him to recognize, let alone commit to memory.

Then, ahead of him through the trees, stronger than the high fading moon, Gallant saw glimmers of yellow light.

Abruptly the trail emerged from the trees, curved again in a wide sweep then dipped towards a rotting timber fence enclosing the grounds of a single-storey ranch house. Oil lamps turned windows and door into warm rectangles, the light faintly illuminating a rickety windmill and the walls of neglected outbuildings.

Gallant realized at once that he could proceed no further without revealing his presence. He drew his horse into the trees, then walked it over crackling dead branches to a position from where he could see without being seen.

Wilson Teager and his companion rode down the slope, through the big open gate and into the yard. Now, with the light touching and dying against the dull black of their black clothing, they were clearly recognizable. It was a ride of some fifty yards. Teager took the lead. The sound of their horses' hoofs announced their arrival. As Gallant watched with interest, three men came out of the house to meet the outlaws.

Gents, Gallant thought. No ruffians, those.

By the glowing light of the oil lamps he saw that these men bore the stamp of wealth. They were tall, erect, arrogant. On one of them, dark hair shone lustrously; on the others tanned scalps shone though hair which had thinned. And across tight-stretched vests that were revealed by the unbuttoned jackets of black suits, gold watch chains glittered.

The perpetrators, Gallant decided with conviction. Wealthy businessmen by the looks of them, but these were the men behind the mischief, without a doubt. All he had to discover now was what form that mischief took, and what the hell it was they'd perpetrated.

SIX

Life, Born Gallant philosophized, was full of surprises. In the same instant he found himself thanking his lucky stars that it should be so. Without surprises, he reasoned, without a bracing shock every now and then to insert steel into the wilting spine, life wouldn't be worth the candle.

'What do you think, old son?' he said.

The man was sitting on Gallant's bed in the hotel on the outskirts of Kansas City. His back was against the faded wallpaper. Across his lap was resting what looked to Gallant very much like a '73 Winchester. He knew there was a shell in the breech, knew damn well the muzzle was pointing in his direction. Teager's Peacemaker was tucked in his waistband, but caution ruled and he was making no sudden movements.

'You tell me,' the man said, unmoved.

'Funny,' Gallant said, resting his back against the thin door, 'but back there in Tancred's saloon when

56

you directed me to Millie's dairy I had you pegged for a scared rabbit.'

'Maybe I am, and maybe I'm not,' said the man with the rifle, 'but I do know a good story when I smell it.'

'Ah,' Gallant said, with a gleam of understanding. 'You're a man with ink-stained fingers and a green eye shade, out on a moonlit night chasing a scoop.'

'Got it. I'm Stick McCrae, of the *Kansas City Star*.'

'Stick?'

'I started work as a compositor.'

'Letterpress printing,' Gallant said, nodding knowingly as he turned a little to one side as if to find comfort but used the move to let his hand inch its way towards the Peacemaker. 'You used a composing stick to assemble the type, and the name stuck.'

McCrae grinned. 'Well said. The job called for keen eyes, concentration and dexterity. Those talents are ingrained, and I'll use every one of them if you touch that big six-gun.'

'Wouldn't dream of it,' Gallant said, moving into the room and dragging out a straight chair to straddle. 'Used up all my luck back there in the Last Chance. My daddy always told me a man's best asset was knowing when to stop.'

'Did he include talking?'

'If he did you're in for a rough time. You're after a story, and I won't be much good to you with a buttoned lip.'

After leaving the isolated ranch Gallant had

retraced his route along the trail winding through the woods, circled around the festering hole that was Salvation Creek and made his way in a leisurely manner back to Kansas City. The night was pleasantly warm. For most of the long ride he'd been deep in thought as he rocked sleepily to the movements of his patient horse, but strive as he might to make sense out of chaos it had turned out to be an exercise in futility.

Nothing he squeezed out of the sponge that was his overworked brain brought him any enlightenment – which was hardly surprising. Since leaving William Pinkerton a couple of days before he'd been hired by the devious Max Tremblay, emerged unbloodied from a one-sided knock-down brawl with Wilson Teager and his partner, gazed from afar at businessmen he'd shrewdly judged to be the brains behind ... behind what? There lay the problem. Those well-fed men in their expensive suits might be the brains, but what it was they were behind was a mystery to Gallant.

And so, with very little to show for his night's work, he returned to Kansas City.

Deep thinking plays havoc with the fine-tuned alertness essential to staying alive in the West, or anywhere else, for that matter, as Gallant had learned from his experiences with the British Army in India. Nevertheless, his guard had slipped. Still bogged down in a mire of implausible theories, he had opened the door to his room, stepped inside, and been jerked back to reality by the metallic clack of a weapon being cocked. McCrae had nodded politely in greeting, but the Winchester's barrel glinted wickedly in the light of the oil lamp. Gallant had been caught cold, and by a man he at first glance did not recognize.

The gaunt and fearful creature he had spoken to at the entrance to Tancred's saloon had been transformed into a whip-thin individual with keen eyes, steady hands and, apparently, nerves of steel. His garb was ordinary – he'd taken off a shabby jacket and exposed army suspenders and sleeve gaiters – but Gallant was impressed by the cool competence of his demeanour.

There was also a full measure of patience in the man, Gallant thought now. McCrae had broken into his room – well, walked in, because Gallant hadn't locked it – he was after a story, and he was prepared to wait. But if McCrae could smell a story, then surely he was better informed than Gallant? A spell of listening was on the cards, Gallant decided. Let the newspaper man do most of the talking. Wear his patience so thin he gets careless.

McCrae, he realized, was watching him with amusement. Without warning, the newspaper man slid the rifle off his lap and stood up. He stretched, yawned, walked a few weary paces one way across the bare room, then back again.

'I've read Tremblay's notes,' he said. He picked the sheet of paper off the table, flapped it. 'Knowing Wilson Teager's reputation, I'd say Tremblay handed you a hastily scrawled death warrant. How did you see it?'

'A way in,' Gallant said. 'That's why I went to Tremblay.'

'No. You went because William Pinkerton sent you.'

'If you know that, then you also know why.'

'I'd say that was obvious. His Kansas office honcho was murdered. He wants the killer brought to justice.'

'That's part of it.'

McCrae waited for more. Gallant held his tongue.

McCrae cocked his head. 'So what about the killing? You got Teager down for that?'

'That's where it gets tricky. Tremblay as good as told me Teager pulled the trigger. If he knew that for sure, it means one of two things.'

McCrae nodded. 'Either Tremblay's a clever investigator loyal to Pinkerton, or he's involved in the killings.'

'And there's only one of those reasons that justifies sending me, an unarmed tenderfoot, after Wilson Teager.'

McCrae was sitting on the windowsill, arms folded. Gallant watched him reach across to pull the makings from his jacket and begin rolling a cigarette. The thin hands nimbly sprinkled tobacco on the brown paper. Behind him, filthy net curtains were moving gently in the draught from the open window. He looked up, caught Gallant's gaze.

'You said finding the killer was just one of the reasons why Pinkerton sent you to Tremblay.'

'Did I?'

'Indeed you did. And I think I know why you're playing your cards close to your chest.' He nodded slowly. 'Yeah, you *and* Pinkerton. Admit it, Gallant, the pair of you haven't a clue what's going on. You're waiting for me to dig you out of a hole.'

'You could make a start by explaining tonight. You got to Last Chance before me. How'd that happen?'

'Pure luck. I'd come across a name, and it was linked to a story I was following. I found out where this man, a Texan cattleman, was staying—'

'The ranch out there in the middle of nowhere to the south of Salvation Creek?'

'That's right. It's the Taylor spread, Broken T, fitting title because it's empty and run down. Len Taylor's an old man now, he lives in town and the place is up for sale. He's probably grateful for the few dollars' rent he's getting paid while he waits.'

'And. . . ?'

'When I got to the Broken T, I made damn sure I approached with caution. The moon made that difficult, but it was just as well I took care. I was expecting one horse, but saw three in the corral and that warned me to stay back in the trees. Way it worked out, it was as close as I needed to get. Even from more'n a hundred yards I could see three men in the big living room. One big man in a suit was talking to a couple of rough looking characters; I assume he was the gent I was supposed to be meeting. Teager I recognized from the beard. The other was Tyne Messner, he's served time for robbery – and, I tell you, seeing those two gunnies there was a shock.'

'Why?'

'It changed everything.' McCrae shrugged, but didn't elaborate. 'The gent in the suit was agitated, walking up and down, oil lamps casting shadows everywhere as he spread his hands and shrugged his shoulders. The way I read it, Teager was questioning him, the businessman was getting angry because he couldn't come up the answers.'

'Then Teager and this Messner rode out—'

'And I hung on to their tails.' McCrae nodded.

'Yes, well, we both know you finished up in Salvation Creek, so let's skip that bit. Tell me, why were you so interested in this cattleman that you'd ride forty miles or more from Kansas City to talk to him?'

'Arn Wakeman? The answer to that,' McCrae said, 'is all tied in with his reason for hiring a couple of outlaws.'

'Which you're going to keep to yourself.'

'For now.'

'A minute ago you said Teager and Messner being there at the Broken T changed everything. But it's changed again since then, hasn't it – or is that something I know and you don't?'

'You tell me.'

'Your favourite three words. I guess it's the news-paperman in you, forcing the other man to talk. All right. I followed Teager and Messner when they rode back to Broken T. Like you, I stayed back in the woods. And I can tell you, your lone cattleman has got himself two companions.'

'Yeah, I know. You followed the two gunnies, I followed you.'

'Jesus, it's a wonder we weren't all bumping into each other!' Gallant grinned at the man's persistence. 'So what about those two newcomers at the Broken T? Have they got a place in that story you were following?'

'I reckon their arrival wraps up the first phase. From here on in, things could get rough.'

'As if they haven't already.'

'You and Teager?' It was McCrae's turn to grin. 'I was impressed.'

'The feeling's mutual. You've been running around like a chicken with no head, but still got back here before I did. How did that happen?'

'Earlier in the day I picked up your sign and followed you from the Pinkertons' offices. I knew you were using this flea pit. It was easy enough to outpace you on the ride back from Broken T.' He shook his head. 'The way it's been going, I feel like I've been following one man or another for most of a day and night.'

'Final question,' Gallant said, standing up and kicking the straight chair back against the table. 'Teager and Messner. Are they also holed up at Broken T?'

'No sir, they're not,' McCrae said. 'They have a shack back there in that hellhole called Salvation Creek. And when I said things could get rough, I wasn't kidding. Teager and Messner are not alone.

Tonight, you were lucky. There's another couple of hard characters there. Along with Teager and Messner, they make up a formidable foursome.'

SEVEN

'Who the hell was that smooth talking gent? He near took my head off at the shoulders – and he had a smile on his face as he clubbed me with my own damn six-gun.'

'I have no idea,' Arn Wakeman said. 'A stranger passing through the Creek, he took a dislike to your face—'

'No.' Wilson Teager shook his head emphatically. 'He knew too much; he knew everything; knew I'd gunned down the Pinkertons' office honcho, knew I'd winged William Pinkerton.'

The bearded outlaw was sitting at the dusty table across from Tyne Messner in old Len Taylor's dilapidated Broken T ranch house. He was talking through the bloodstained bandanna he held to his mouth. His jaw was swollen, but not broken. He was missing several teeth; others, broken off close to the gum, had sharp edges that were cutting painfully into his cheek.

Tyne Messner, a glass of whiskey in his hand, was

nodding agreement.

'Asked for Teager by name,' he said. 'An Englishman playing the damn fool, and, Christ, didn't we fall for it.'

Arn Wakeman was frowning as he looked away from the outlaws, and across the room at the two listening businessmen. Both had removed their black jackets and unbuttoned their vests. They were on either side of the cold stone fireplace, sitting in old armchairs with split seams and exposed stuffing. Legs outstretched, his red face glistening, Benny Callan was puffing on a fat cigar. Steve Farrell was leaning forward, elbows on spread knees. A whiskey glass was held loosely in his hand, but his eyes were speculative as he met Wakeman's gaze.

'Me and Benny, we arrived here today, by train from Amarillo, then horseback from Kansas City. We're tired – and we get here, we're hit by this nonsense. You came on ahead, Arn, set it all up, yet it seems the only people who know what's going on are these two gunnies.'

'Forget that line of thinking,' Teager said, shifting so that his remaining six-gun rattled against the chair as he growled menacingly. 'We've kept tight- lipped, said nothing out of place, let nothing slip. Grant and Hayes back in Salvation Creek, all they know is, like us, they're hired guns. Only thing interests them is the money.'

'You didn't let me finish,' Farrell said equably. 'I was going to ask about Max Tremblay. According to you, Arn, he's a glorified office boy with no future, suddenly elevated to a position of power. He knows about Consolidated, knows we're out to scupper the deal, knows how we intend doing it. So what's your honest opinion? Could he have something to do with this Gallant character? Is Tremblay to be trusted?'

'I believe he'll keep his mouth shut, because he's terrified of men like Teager and Messner. But he's no bright spark, he's in that office on his own, and without someone watching over him—'

'Can't see it,' Benny Callan cut in. 'Like these two here, Tremblay's in it for the money. OK, he's stupid, but he knows Teager here's one of the men playing a key role in this whole affair. Teager and his pals, they're the men going to guarantee him a big payout by getting rid of James Lake. Why would he send this feller Gallant all the way down to Salvation Creek?'

'I don't know, and I can't say I care,' Wakeman said, 'because I believe we're giving too much importance to a violent incident that has done nothing to disrupt our plans. There's one man out there, Born Gallant, and he's struck a blow but is left chasing shadows. We've got two days, but we don't need a quarter of that time if we can get this finished tonight.'

'Tonight's over, dead and gone,' Teager said.

'No. You ride now you can hit Rocking L before dawn. Bad time for them. Cold, half asleep, Lake'll be a sitting duck.'

'What about ranch-hands. How many wire-tough cowboys are there, happy to join in the fun and spoil the party?'

'It's fall roundup. At most there's two or three lame and lazy left behind. You'll be in and out before they come tumbling out of the bunkhouse.'

'Sounds reasonable,' Teager said, 'but we're the men taking the risks and there's still questions begging for answers.'

'Just the one,' Wakeman said. 'You asked about Born Gallant, the honest answer was we don't know who he is, what he was doing in Salvation Creek.'

'Or are you wondering why Lake has to die, Teager?' Farrell drained his whiskey and stood up, a big man with the swell of his stomach straining the buttons on his white shirt. 'Well, here's my answer. You've got a job to do, and the less you know about it, the less your conscience is going to bother you when the bullets slam home.'

'Conscience never did figure large in my life,' Teager said, 'and as for Gallant, I'll deal with him in my own way, when the time comes. But he wasn't alone, so now I'm asking about the girl.'

Wakeman frowned. 'What girl?'

'Young woman in Salvation Creek who put herself between Gallant and the pursuit and held them off till he was clear. Fired a rifle from horseback like a Sioux brave. Rode a pint-sized cayuse with the speed of a thoroughbred, and when last seen she'd caught Gallant and they were riding together.'

'Then my answer's the same,' Wakeman said dismissively. 'I don't know him, I don't know her, it remains an incident that's left us untouched.'

'It's a warning,' Tyne Messner said. 'Only a fool

68

would ignore it.'

'Then move fast, before they can act,' Wakeman said bluntly. 'Go now to Salvation Creek, roust Grant and Hayes from their blankets, the four of you ride on to the Rocking L and get this finished. You want your money. I want James Lake dead – and I want him dead before daybreak.'

'Where have you been?'

James Lake was staring at his daughter, his eyes painfully narrowed, in them the hard glint of barely suppressed fear. She had walked into the Rocking L ranch house out of the ghostly half light that preceded the dawn, bringing with her a chill aura of danger that enveloped her like a cold shroud. Her lustrous dark hair was dulled and tangled, her clothing snagged by thorns, her cotton shirt sweat-stained. She was clutching her Winchester rifle with a white-knuckled grip, but the fire of an indomitable resolve burned in her bright blue eyes and the look she gave her father was at once challenging, and serene.

'Saving your life, Pa. Is it all right for me to do that?'

'It's not all right, because there's no need. I've no idea what you're talking about.'

Rebecca, her hands clasped, was standing by the desk next to her husband.

'We've been worried sick,' she said softly. 'Your pa's right. I don't know what makes you think his life's in danger.'

'Yes, you do,' Melody said. 'Both of you.'

69

Lake laughed harshly, but the naked apprehension in his eyes had been replaced by wariness. 'You're talking nonsense. I don't know where you've been, but to make us your excuse—'

'I've overheard you talking,' Melody said, and she looked accusingly at them from beneath raised eyebrows.

There was a stunned silence.

'I'll . . . I'll make us all a hot drink,' Rebecca said, 'while you explain that unacceptable behaviour to your father.'

'You know what I mean, don't you?' Melody said when the door had closed behind her mother. She leaned the rifle against the gun cabinet, ran her fingers through her hair, smoothed her clothing with her hands. 'And what I do is not unacceptable, because this is my family and I don't like being kept in the dark. You talk at night, when you think I'm in bed. About something called Consolidated, about a consortium, about you being the driving force behind some merger that's going to take place; how, without you, it's doomed to failure.'

'It's cattle business, Melody. We succeed, or we fail. But business failure is not a matter of life and death.'

He was leaning back against the desk, legs crossed, arms folded. His tone was reassuring, but it was belied by the haunted expression in eyes sunken with strain.

'I told you I've been listening,' Melody said.

Lake smiled. 'You must have misheard—'

'Oh, for God's sake—'

'Melody!'

'Yes, all right, but you'd make a man of the cloth swear like a mule-skinner. I've heard you. Do you understand? Very little you and Ma have discussed has escaped my notice. I know that men are gunning for you – or will be soon, because there's some sort of deadline and time's running out. There are rich men, Texans, with too much to lose. They believe that removing you will solve their immediate problems. What's the word I've heard you use? Linchpin? That's you, isn't it – only it's not. You're supposed to be the all-powerful rancher without whom this . . . deal . . . falls flat. But that's not you at all. You're the deer tied in the clearing waiting for the circling wolves to move in and tear you to shreds. You're bait, Pa, a lawyer turned small rancher now raised to false prominence to protect the men who really matter – and for that you're going to die.'

James Lake took a deep breath. Neither he nor his daughter spoke for a while. They were listening to the clatter of dishes in the kitchen; listening to the silence wherein hung the enormity of what Melody had laid bare before them with a few stark, chilling words.

'Do you know anything at all about Consolidated?' Lake said at last.

'Nothing. I've spoken to Granddad. He knows as much as me. But Granddad does know what I was trying to do tonight, he knows why I was taking such an enormous risk, and he's backing me to the hilt.'

'Yes,' Lake said quietly and with pride, 'Pa would do that.'

'He knew where I was going. I told him not to tell you.'

'And where was that?'

'Salvation Creek.'

'Why there?'

'I know a man in Kansas City. A newspaperman called McCrae. He interviewed me once about my law studies – you'll remember the article in the *Star*. Well, he'd heard something about hired guns, knew where they were holed up.'

'My God, Melody,' Lake said. 'And on the word of a newspaperman you went to Salvation Creek gunning for outlaws?'

Without waiting for an answer he crossed swiftly to the gun cabinet, snatched up the Winchester before Melody could stop him, put the muzzle to his nose and sniffed.

'Damn it, Melody, this has been fired.'

'Yes.'

'Have you killed a man?'

'Possibly. We were being pursued, first out of Salvation Creek, then across open prairie.'

'We?'

'There was a man in the saloon owned by a 'breed called Sundown Tancred. I was looking for a villain, Wilson Teager, but a devil-may-care Englishman called Born Gallant got there before me.' She grinned, her eyes sparkling. 'In front of mean looking characters, armed to the teeth, he made a bloody mess of Teager's bearded face and got clean away. It was a swift departure that only just got him clear of a howling mob.' She shrugged. 'Or as close as you can get to a mob in a reeking settlement like Salvation Creek.'

'Where is he now?'

'Gallant?' Melody grimaced, her eyes at once hopeful and despairing. 'I wish I knew. We split up, and I'm beginning to think that was a bad idea. If I'm going to save your life I need all the help I can get.'

'No.' Lake lay the rifle carefully on the desk, his face set. 'This stops now, Melody. I've no intention of hiding behind my daughter. Anyway, Creed and Lancing arrive tomorrow. With three of us here in the house the odds swing in our favour.' He thought for a moment, then his face lightened. 'Besides, didn't you say this feller Gallant dealt with that bearded outlaw? I'm assuming the newspaperman McCrae gave you Teager's name because he's top dog. So with him badly beaten by this Gallant the others will be without a leader, they'll lose heart, slink away. . . .'

'Beaten for a man like Wilson Teager is a long way from being finished, Pa. And from what I understand, Creed and Lancing are ranchers used to living off the fat of the land, not gunmen driven by desperation. I can't see them being of much help in a tight spot.' She paused, her brow furrowed with thought. 'What time do you expect them here?'

'Impossible to say.' Lake shrugged. 'They'll hire a couple of horses or a buggy in town. I can't see them getting here before the afternoon.'

Melody smiled wryly. 'And it's not yet dawn. I was going to stay at Granddad's place tonight, but I'm glad I didn't—'

'Oh, come on,' Lake scoffed, 'you're seeing danger where none exists, your bearded gunslinger's rolled in his blankets licking his wounds and—'

He broke off. Startled, he swung towards the window.

'What the hell was that?'

'That,' Melody said, 'is a bunch of horsemen, crossing the yard towards the house.'

Moving with grace and speed, she sprang forward, swept the Winchester off the desk and made for the door.

beating a tattoo on the packed dirt of the yard as he spoke. The four riders were advancing in line abreast, slowing now, Teager and Messner flanked by Grant and Hayes. Still forty yards from the house, the two outriders began moving way out to the side to present difficult targets and be in a position to send down a withering crossfire.

Even as the line became spaced out, the house door banged open. A young woman stood outlined in the opening, a stark silhouette against the warm yellow lamplight. She was holding a rifle. Its steely glitter sent an instant chill of apprehension through the approaching riders. No warning was given before she fired. In the wan light the vivid spurt of orange flame was shockingly intense, searing to the eyes. It was followed instantly by the whip-like crack of the shot. Messner grunted as if slammed in his middle by a hard punch. He slumped forward in the saddle, then toppled sideways to flop like a heavy rag doll on the hard ground. His horse, head tossing and eyes rolling white, pawed the air with flailing forelegs then veered sharply to its left and almost unseated Teager as bay and sorrel collided weightily.

The second bullet whistled over Teager's head as he fought to control his mount. The sorrel whirled on dancing hoofs, spun dizzily, and Teager found himself facing back the way they had come. He hauled on the reins, twisted his neck to see two men in dark pants and off-white undershirts come tumbling from the bunkhouse. Shocked and fearful, they yelled something Teager didn't catch, then hastily threw themselves back inside the low-slung building and slammed the door as Hayes opened up on them with his six-gun.

Still fighting his spooked horse, Teager saw the young woman pull back inside the house and push the door to. Messner was an inert dark heap in the centre of the yard. Hayes was out of the saddle and had slipped into the cover of the bunkhouse's end wall. Then there was the startling tinkle of breaking glass, repeated as from inside the house a second window was deliberately smashed. Rifle barrels were poked between jagged shards of glass. Again a rifle opened up. Another bullet whined close to Teager and, back in control, reins taut in his gloved grasp, he ducked low and spurred the trembling sorrel into a furious gallop towards the big open barn on the left of the yard.

Grant tore ahead of him. They pounded straight into gloom and the sweet dry smell of hay, tumbled from their saddles. There was the smooth whisper of leather as both men slid rifles from saddle boots, then slapped their horses' rumps to send them away into the barn's dark depths.

'I guess I got my answer,' Teager said grimly, hugging the timber wall by the opening so he was sheltered but had a clear view of the house.

Grant, a stocky man in rough range clothing, wearing a sweat-stained hat with its front brim pinned up with a sliver of bone, was down on one knee with his rifle.

'You saying, yeah, they can hold us off?'

'I'm saying I now know who the young woman was back at Salvation Creek.'

'I don't know anything about that,' Grant said, 'but if Messner out there was still breathing he'd tell you for certain she's a crack shot.'

'And now there's two of them with rifles,' Teager said thoughtfully, 'that young woman and her pa.' He spat sideways, wiped his beard and stared at the blood on the back of his hand. 'They'll have a gun cabinet in there, which gives them more than one rifle apiece. If Lake's wife reloads for them there'll be no let up in their firing.'

'I can make it all the way over there,' Grant said, 'if you fire regular, punch lead through those windows, keep their heads down. I get close to that wall they can't touch me 'less they lean out – and they won't be doing that.'

Teager's grin was savage. 'There's wide flowerbeds there, the lady of the house has prepared soft ground so's you can hunker down in comfort. Leave me your rifle. You'll have your Colt, I'll have enough shells to pin them down till you and Hayes make it.'

He shifted his position, waved across the yard to where Hayes was leaning with his back up against the bunkhouse's end wall. The other man acknowledged with a lifted hand. But Teager had been careless. Again the rifle cracked. The bullet thudded into the woodwork close to the bearded outlaw's face. Sharp splinters were like needles piercing his forehead. He swore crudely, ducked back with tears of pain leaking from his eyes.

Swiftly, from the safety of shadows, Teager used urgent gestures to make clear to the man by the bunkhouse what he and Grant planned. It required several attempts. Finally, Hayes understood. He nodded, gave Teager the thumbs up, hitched his gunbelt and wiped the palms of his hands on his pants.

'When you reach the house,' Teager told Grant, 'you and Hayes cover for me and I'll follow. You say the Lakes daren't risk showing themselves, but fear can turn a mild and sensible man into a hero, or a fool. Edge as close as you can get to the windows, poke your hand over the sill and fire blind into the house to make damn sure they stay down.' He looked at Grant, got a nod of understanding, and said, 'OK, then get ready and move when I commence firing. And when you're running, stay out wide so you don't stop any of my flying lead.'

With Grant's rifle lying ready in the scattered straw by his boots, Teager dropped to one knee and slammed the butt of his own rifle into his shoulder. Blood from skin broken by the flying splinters was trickling down his forehead. Angrily he dashed it away. He drew a bead on the window to the left of the door, and squeezed the trigger; shifted his aim to the other window and fired a second shot, grinning as he heard a faint yell of alarm.

Even as Teager's heavy bullets plucked at the curtains, Grant was off, heading for the house in a crouching, swerving run. Across the yard, Hayes left the shelter of the bunkhouse, but ran straight and true and was already closing in on the house as Teager fired his carefully spaced third and fourth shots. When his fifth and sixth shots hissed through the shattered windows and slammed into the living-room's rear wall both Grant and Hayes had finished their runs and flopped down, kicking up soft earth and crushing flowers and shrubs as they set their backs hard up against the ranch house's log walls.

Teager tilted his Winchester, gave a nod to the watching Grant, waited.

Grant twisted awkwardly, lifted his right arm and blasted a shot over the windowsill and into the room. As the echoes of the shot faded, Hayes, on the other side of the door, rose up on his knees and pumped two fast shots over the sill. There was the tinkle of broken pottery. A squeal of feminine dismay came from inside the house.

Then Wilson Teager was up on his feet and running, a Winchester rifle clutched in each hand.

Yet even as he ran, his mind raced ahead of him and his skin crawled with the dreadful anticipation of a fatal shot that would end his life. He knew that shooting blind had its drawbacks. From their positions beneath the windows Grant and Hayes were doing little more than drill holes in the ceiling. To do even that, they were taking risks.

Teager, heart thundering, was less than halfway to the house when Grant stretched up too high trying for a better shot. Someone inside the room had anticipated the move. They chopped down from the side of the window with a rifle barrel. The outlaw's wrist snapped like a dry stick. He let out a howl of agony. His six-gun fell from deadened fingers. He crumpled into the soil, moaning and clutching his arm.

At once a figure holding a rifle loomed in the window. Teager was exposed, caught out in the open. He swore through gritted teeth. The rifle cracked. Hot lead plucked at his sleeve. Teager roared mightily in angry frustration, jinked left, then right – and ran straight into the second shot. His hat flew from his head. He heard death's mocking whisper as the bullet parted his hair. His mouth gaped. He sucked in gasping breaths. A third shot cracked. It clipped the heel from his boot. His next step was unbalanced. He staggered and almost went down. Then he had reached the house. He dived for the wall. The shock as he was brought to a jolting stop against the massive logs sent waves of agony through his injured face. One arm went numb. He dropped Grant's rifle, painfully jacked a shell into the breech of his own Winchester. He swung it one-handed up towards the window, desperately pulled the trigger.

As the deafening roar of the shot died away, a leaden silence settled over house and yard. Both factions paused to draw breath, but the advantage had shifted to the Broken L defenders. Messner was dead, Grant out of the fight, and Teager knew the situation was close to a Mexican stand off. The defenders were trapped in the house. He and Hayes were as good as pinned against the outside wall, hunkered down in the only available cover.

81

But the cover they had, Teager quickly realized, gave them a winning advantage. What Grant had pointed out still held true: the defenders could not shoot at the men outside unless they poked their heads out of those windows. He and Hayes, on the other hand, could move freely if they remained close to the walls, the door was midway between them and just a couple of strides away – and the thin shaft of lamplight showing yellow in the dust told Teager it was still a little way open. A little would be more than enough.

Teager scrambled to his knees, then up on to his feet. He flattened himself against the wall, squinted sideways at Hayes. The outlaw was watching, waiting, six-gun up and ready. Teager pointed, indicating the door. He bunched his fists up by his chest and made a fierce show of barging sideways with his shoulder. Hayes nodded quickly, eyes bright splinters of light. Teager put down the Winchester and drew his six-gun. He raised his left hand, showed three fingers. Again Hayes nodded.

Teager moved a little way from the wall, turned to face the door. He took a deep breath. His mouth was filled with the coppery taste of blood. His broken teeth were jagged. Where the man Gallant had struck him in the fight at Salvation Creek his face ached fiercely. But none of that mattered. His bearded countenance split in a wolfish grin. Again he raised his hand, this time as a warning to Hayes to get ready. Then he brought it down once, twice, and a third time – and lunged for the door.

Hayes moved like a bronc exploding from a rodeo

chute, and got there before him. He hit the door with the full weight of his short, stocky body behind his shoulder. The door, the catch not engaged, swung inwards without resistance. Hayes was taken by surprise. His boot snagged on the step. He tumbled into the room, rolling to one side as Teager charged in after him. The bearded outlaw leaped over the fallen Hayes, took three long strides then spun to face the windows and dropped to a crouch with his six-gun extended.

Two women were staring at him. An older woman with flecks of grey in her hair whom he took to be Lake's wife was standing with her back against the front wall. She was holding a rifle, but it was slack in her hands and her eyes were wide with fright. At the other window a younger woman with rich dark hair and eyes that were sparkling pools of excitement was grinning at him along the steady barrel of a Winchester.

'Drop it,' Teager snarled.

'Ha,' the young woman mocked. 'Have you looked in a mirror, seen your face? I was there, remember? You weren't up to much at Salvation Creek, and you'll fare no better here.'

'Drop it now,' Teager said, straightening from his crouch and shifting his aim as Hayes climbed to his feet, 'or I'll plant a six-gun slug between your mother's breasts.'

'No you won't. Outlaws are cowards. You know that if you shoot my mother, your next breath will be your last.'

'Leave it to me—'

Hayes stepped forward, voice raised angrily, and there was a metallic snap as he thumbed back the hammer of his six-gun. Teager stepped across quickly, held him back with an outstretched arm. He could see the young woman's forefinger curled around the rifle's trigger. The knuckle was white. He felt his skin prickle.

'You'd risk your mother's life,' he said quickly, 'on a snap judgement of my character?'

'You talk well, but that's all it is. Empty talk. There is no risk. You're too yellow to pull the trigger, Teager, because for the second time tonight you're staring certain death in the face.'

'Where's your pa?'

'In town. In a hotel in Kansas City.'

'You're lying.'

She smiled mysteriously. 'Am I? Perhaps you're right. Perhaps he's standing behind you now, in the open kitchen doorway, a rifle aimed at your back.'

'He's not,' Hayes snapped, risking a glance.

'All right,' the young woman acknowledged, 'so you've looked. But you can only see so far. The door's closed, isn't it? – but couldn't he be on the other side, waiting?'

'Go search the house,' Teager growled.

And now the girl laughed openly. 'You think your man will go over and open that door? You think he's brave enough? Because you can't tell lies from truth now, can you? Is James Lake in Kansas City, or is he over there behind that door—'

'Hayes will go where I tell him, damn it—'

'And what? You'll hold us here with your one remaining Peacemaker? Oh, and by the way, where is the other one? Does a bold Englishman called Gallant have it in his possession?' Then, as Teager's battered face flushed with shame and fury, she seemed to relent. 'Oh, for goodness' sake, off you go, little man, and look around,' she told Hayes. 'And when you discover I'm telling the truth, you can both get the hell out of here and leave us in peace.'

A door banged as the stocky outlaw left the room. Teager guessed there'd be a kitchen, a couple of bedrooms, perhaps a storeroom, a back porch. In the main ranch house there'd be nowhere else Lake could be hiding. That left the barn, and the bunkhouse – and it was one thing to drive frightened men back inside, another thing entirely to go in there and dig them out so the place could be searched.

Besides, any search beyond those four walls was a futile waste of time. If Lake wasn't in the house, he could be anywhere on several thousand acres of property. And Teager had two men, and one of those injured. . . .

Suddenly, standing there, Teager felt foolish. The girl was openly amused. The rifle she held had not wavered. He had witnessed the accuracy of her shooting back in Salvation Creek, and in this very yard, and was under no illusions. If she pulled the trigger from point blank range, he would die – and all the money Wakeman, Callan and Farrell could rain

85

down on him would be no compensation.

Suddenly Hayes was back in the room. Teager flashed him a glance. Hayes shook his head.

'She's telling the truth. He's not here.'

'He's in Kansas City,' The girl said. 'I *told* you—'

'I'm Rebecca Lake, James Lake's wife,' the older woman cut in. They were the first words she had spoken. There was a pink flush of colour warming once pale cheeks. She had moved away from her position against the wall. As she approached Teager the rifle was held more firmly, its aim clear. 'What do you want with my husband?'

'We have a business proposition for him,' Teager said warily.

'Really? But you attacked us. You stormed our house.'

Teager shook his head. 'No. You're forgetting what happened. We rode in openly. Your daughter fired on us without warning as we approached. A man is dead. She's guilty of murder.'

Rebecca seemed to hesitate, but her look was scornful. 'And after that, here in this room, you didn't threaten to . . . to shoot me?'

'I was angry. The proposition is important, time is short. I need to put it to Lake. He can take it, or leave it. Up to him.'

'And what would you have done,' Rebecca said, 'if you'd put it to him and he'd rejected it?'

'Taken his decision to the people I'm working for,' Teager said, 'which is where I'm going now. They won't be too pleased. You can expect another visit, when your husband's here.'

He looked at Hayes, saw the resignation in the stocky outlaw's eyes, and shrugged. Then, always aware of the two rifles that seemed to be following him like the accusing eyes of a particularly ugly oil painting, Wilson Teager strode across the room and followed Hayes out of the Broken H.

The dignity of his departure was ruined by his broken heel, which made him walk like a lame horse wrangler the worse for drink. Also, he tried to slam the door behind him. But as if to demonstrate the sheer incompetence he had brought to everything he had encountered that evening, the door hit the jamb, and bounced open.

'You see now why I went to Salvation Creek,' Melody Lake said.

James Lake frowned. He was sipping hot coffee. As soon as the outlaws had ridden from the yard, Rebecca had pulled aside the rugs from the back porch floor and, with Melody's help, opened the heavy trap door leading to the storm cellars. Lake had climbed the ladder without speaking. No man, Rebecca knew, liked hiding behind a woman's skirts, and James Lake had hidden behind two.

'You handled the situation well,' he said now. 'I could hear most of what went on, and I can't believe how brave you both were. But I'm not quite sure what you mean, Melody.'

'Isn't it obvious? Pa, this Consolidated affair – whatever it is – is occupying your every waking

87

minute to the exclusion of everything else. The repair of that front door lock had taken on enormous significance. You knew we were under threat, knew we had to be secure, yet it slipped your mind – if you thought about it at all.'

'Your ma reminded me.'

'And still you did nothing,' Rebecca said. 'If that had been locked and barred—'

'So let's get clear battle lines drawn,' Melody said. 'Pa, for the next day or whatever time's left, you concentrate on business, leave security to me.'

'You're a young woman. You can't go up against those violent men alone.'

'I don't intend to. Once I've had some sleep I'm riding into town. I want to talk to McCrae again.'

'What can he do?'

'I'm hoping,' Melody said with a broad smile, 'that McCrae knows where I can find a certain Englishman with fair hair, blue eyes and several alarming and deadly attributes. If there's one person guaranteed to put the wind up Wilson Teager and his remaining friends, it's Born Gallant.'

PART TWO

THE CATTLEMEN

NINE

'I need your help. Nobody else will do.'

'Golly,' Born Gallant said.

He'd answered the firm rapping on the door to his room to find Melody Lake standing outside. She was dressed in dark trousers tucked into tooled-leather boots, and was wearing a crisp white blouse under a tailored black vest. Her flat crowned grey hat was set on her head at a jaunty angle. Her face was serious, her rich brown eyes warning him that she was in no mood for nonsense.

'The early bird and all that,' Gallant said thoughtfully, 'and I'm the poor worm you're out to catch. Can't argue with that. And straight to the point, too. Very commendable—'

'I was thinking of more appetizing fare,' Melody said, cutting in. 'How about leaving the small talk until we've had breakfast. There's a café nearby.'

'Of course there is, the proprietor knows my fresh face well by now.' He stepped back and adopted a theatrical pose. 'Am I presentable enough for you?'

'You'll do.'

She swung on her heel and headed off down the dingy, green-painted corridor.

'That went down remarkably well,' Gallant mumbled to the wall as he set off after her. 'Wonder what's put her in such a serious mood?'

He didn't get close to finding out until their breakfasts of bacon and eggs had been eaten and the delicious grease mopped from the plates with thick wedges of bread. A thin young woman in a filthy apron made for a man twice her size replaced their empty plates with cups of steaming black coffee, and they sat back and regarded each other with undisguised interest.

Idly stirring sugar into her coffee with a heavy metal spoon, Melody's eyes were amused.

'If you think I was early getting to your room,' she said, 'you should have seen the look on McCrae's face.'

'Didn't know you knew him.'

'We're old pals.'

'Newspapermen have contacts, people they use. They've been known, on the odd occasion, to have parents – but pals?'

'Oh, all right, he wrote a story about me. I've almost finished law studies. Model student, very high marks throughout.'

'And you went to thank him today, at dawn.'

'Stick McCrae knows everything, and I was in a hurry to find you.'

'Lord knows why. All you know about me is that I

hit big men, then run away.'

'The fact that you were able to get out of Salvation Creek at all was what impressed me most.'

'Ah, but you must take most of the credit for that—'

'Last night,' Melody cut in, 'Wilson Teager rode into Broken L with three gunmen. He came to kill my father.'

Gallant pursed his lips. His mild blue eyes had narrowed a little, and now held a steely glint.

'How'd they get on?'

'One man dead, Messner, you met him in the Last Chance. Another has a broken arm. Pa's fine, I made him hide in the cellar. Teager left with his tail between his legs, snarling and licking his wounds.'

'If you can do that much damage to men of Teager's ilk,' Gallant said softly, 'I wonder what you need me for?'

'I didn't tackle them on my own; Ma broke the outlaw's arm with a blow from her rifle; and I need you because time is running out and from now on things are going to get really tough.'

'Strange, that's what Stick McCrae said. He wouldn't explain. I think you should, if you really want my help. And just to show that I know it has to work both ways, I'll come clean first. The late Alan Pinkerton was an old friend of my family. His son, William, rather put me up to this.'

'Damn it, suddenly all becomes clear,' Melody Lake said, her eyes triumphant. 'I remember you saying, when we'd given those men the slip, that our reasons for being in Salvation Creek were connected.'

'Clear as mud, actually,' Gallant said. 'We both know the connection is Wilson Teager, but after that I'm lost. Anyway, I'm all ears, because you're about to tell me why that bearded hellion wants to fill your father full of holes.'

'It's complicated. I've thought for some time that it might be, but the only clue I had was something called Consolidated. My grandpa couldn't help me, and even after coming close to death my pa flatly refused to discuss it. That left Stick McCrae.'

'The man who knows everything. Yes, I thought it might. Did I tell you he was in my room in the early hours? He was secretive, mumbled something about the first phase being over – came to that conclusion after seeing two new men at a place called Broken T when he'd gone looking for someone called Arn Wakeman.'

'I've heard of Wakeman.' Melody's eyes widened. 'So the Texans are using Len Taylor's place as a base.'

'The Texans being. . . ?' Gallant prompted.

'We'll get to them. All this started twelve months ago, early '84, when cattlemen across the United States realized that working together made good sense and decided to get organized. Something along the lines they were considering had already been done on the Cherokee Strip. Anyway, meetings took place in Chicago and St Louis and, predictably, they managed to make a hash of things: instead of forming one organization, they formed two. The names don't matter – National Cattle Growers, National Cattle and Horse Growers, something like that – because this year they're doing the sensible thing and coming together.'

'By forming a single organization,' Gallant said, 'called Consolidated. . . ?'

'Consolidated Cattle Growers Association of the United States. The presidents of the existing organizations that will merge are ranchers called Creed and Lancing. They're arriving here today, by train, and will ride south to stay with my pa.'

'I know the name of the spread, but where is it?'

'Between here and Salvation Creek.'

'Why stay with your pa?'

'He's involved partly because Grandpa turned the Rocking L into a prosperous ranch. Pa now runs the place, and as a rancher he will benefit from something like Consolidated. However, the main reason he's involved is because before he took over Rocking L, he was a highly respected lawyer.'

'There's a lot of lawyers around,' Gallant pointed out, 'most of them practising and so preferable to someone who's been out of the game for a while.'

'Doesn't matter. My pa, James Lake, must have a special quality. According to McCrae, without him this whole merger could flounder on the rocks.' He could see the pride in her eyes as she went on, 'I know he's been working hard for months. He spends hours at his desk, and he's got a briefcase that he never lets out of his sight. It's absolutely stuffed with important papers.'

'Without which,' Gallant surmised, 'this merger couldn't happen?'

She nodded. 'But they're safe in his keeping. And the meeting to form Consolidated and set up its headquarters here in Kansas City will take place a day from now.'

'I love time limits,' Gallant said, grinning. 'Raises the excitement several notches, especially when men wearing black hats and villainous expressions are lurking in the shadows.'

They'd finished their coffee. A big man in a dirty undershirt who must have lent his apron to the young woman was hovering with a blackened coffee pot. Melody waved him away.

'Arn Wakeman is from the Palo Duro area of North Texas. I don't know about his companions. And it's all right your being flippant, but you know from your experiences at Salvation Creek that those three are not doing their own dirty work. Although they're certainly tough enough, and if they're determined to stop Consolidated they may have to step in if Wilson Teager continues to make a fool of himself.'

'It's not entirely poor old Teager's fault, is it?' Gallant's eyes were glowing. 'I hit him when he wasn't looking, so to speak, then last night he came up against a quite extraordinary young woman.'

Melody grinned. Her dark eyes were dancing, her cheeks pink.

'So if we were working side by side,' she said cautiously, 'we'd stand a good chance of getting Pa and his colleagues to the finishing line in one piece?'

'Hand in hand,' Gallant said boldly, 'there's nothing in the world could hope to stop us.'

'You're with me, then?'

'Wild horses couldn't drag me away. Let's ride at once to the Rocking L and tell your pa his troubles are over.'

'You made a mess of it,' Max Tremblay said, puffing cigar smoke. 'I figured that fool Gallant was working for Pinkerton. I sent him down to Salvation Creek so you could finish him off. Instead you come here into my office looking like you've been stomped by an outlaw bronc.'

'I've been stomped before,' Wilson Teager said. 'Those that did the stomping are pushing up daisies.'

'Hmph.' Tremblay removed the cigar from his mouth to spit a shred of tobacco. Teager's eyes darkened.

'Messner's dead. What about the other one, the man with the broken wrist?'

Teager shrugged. 'Grant? Same answer. It's not the first broken bone he's suffered. He's got two hands so it doesn't stop him using a six-gun.'

'All right. Well, the job's exactly the same. One way or another you stop those men getting anywhere near Kansas City. Three of them. Creed and Lancing, and James Lake.'

'We couldn't find Lake. According to his daughter, he's already here in town.'

Tremblay shook his head irritably. 'She fooled you. He'll wait for the others, see strength in numbers. He believes Creed and Lancing are arriving today, then heading down to his spread – the Rocking L. They'll certainly do that – but they got into town last night. That was arranged by the other man with them, Mack Flynn.'

Teager was frowning. 'That's the first I've heard of him. So now there's four to handle.'

'Three.' Tremblay grinned, his moustache a thin quivering line. 'Creed and Lancing are ranchers, they took Flynn on to ride shotgun. But he's being paid by the Texans, so now there's a man on the inside they don't know about. This Flynn, he knows what he's doing. He brought Creed and Lancing north a day early so he'd have time to see me. I talked to him late last night. He's an intelligent man, used to be a Texas Ranger, got clever ideas of his own that could make your job even easier.'

'You going to let me in on the secret?'

'No. For now, Flynn wants this kept under wraps. You head on back to the Taylor spread. When the time comes, Arn Wakeman'll put you in the picture.'

Teager rose, frowning, tugging at his beard.

'What picture? Maybe we don't need Flynn and his plans. I'd put the night's disasters behind me, got it clear in my head how easy it is to get this job done. Within the next day, Creed, Lancing and Lake are forced to head for town. Somewhere along that trail we gun them down from ambush – they don't know what's hit them. But now you tell me there's complications, talk of clever ideas, and I don't like it because a man can get too clever.'

'You don't have to like it. What you like is in there' – Tremblay jerked his thumb at the small iron safe – 'and you'll get paid handsomely when the job's done.'

He leaned across the desk to grind his cigar in the buffalo hoof ashtray. 'What picture, you say? OK, I'll drop you a hint, but don't let on I've said anything, keep it under your hat.' He squinted up at Teager, and his grin was sly. 'Last night, when you rode into Rocking L, that was your first and last visit. You won't be going there again.'

TEN

James Lake was sprawled against a red and yellow blanket draped across a roomy easy chair that was placed close to his desk, his legs crossed at the ankles, a thin cigar smouldering between his fingers. He was clearly relaxed, at ease. Though the evidence was there in the shattered windows and the bullet holes in the back wall, there was nothing in Lake's rich brown eyes to suggest to the three men watching him that he and his family had only hours ago beaten off a raid by a band of outlaws.

Nor should there be, Lake thought. He was experiencing a feeling close to elation after emerging unscathed from the night's experiences. Then, the arrival of the two ranchers far earlier than expected had been a pleasant surprise that further raised his spirits. Their presence in his house was positive proof that together they were nearing the end of a perilous journey. Over the months his skills as a lawyer, resurrected and dusted off after several years of neglect, had ironed out the many bumps along the negotiation path. Now there were just a couple of days to go and, with Consolidated firmly in place, ranch life would return to normal.

'Thankfully,' Lake said, 'my daughter Melody inherited more than my good looks.' He grinned. 'Along with the intelligence, she also soaked up a good measure of the grit and determination my wife has always shown in everything she has done in life. Indeed, last night Rebecca was standing shoulder to shoulder with Melody, never flinching as bullets whistled past her head.' He turned to look towards the inner door. 'Broke a man's arm, didn't you, Becky? Pointing his six-gun at you, just about to pull the trigger – then crack.'

'He was pointing it at the ceiling,' Rebecca called from the kitchen in a bored voice. 'Honestly, Jim, if you want my opinion I don't think we were ever in any danger.'

Lake rolled his eyes, but the smile that Rebecca could not see was full of pride.

'Nevertheless,' said Henry Lancing, a plump man sitting nervously on the edge of his chair, 'hearing what we're up against makes me wonder if we were wise to come all this way out of Kansas City. The meeting's in town. Surely we'd be safer there, invisible amidst those crowds of people?'

'I agree,' Arthur Creed said. He was standing with his hips against the table, tugging at a grey dragoon moustache. 'Jim, those papers you've been working on are like gold dust; without them, we're lost, and surely they'd be more secure in a hotel safe?'

'They never leave my side,' Lake said, dropping

his hand to pat the worn leather briefcase that rested against his chair.

Creed, noting the movement, shook his head.

'I'm still not convinced this is the safest place. OK, we've got weapons with us' – he slapped a palm on the shiny six-gun in its stiff leather holster – 'but Henry and I, we're no gunslingers. We're getting on in years, too comfortable to retain the hardness of our youth. That's why we brought Mack along with us – but one man can only do so much.'

'It was never going to be just one man,' Lake said. 'I've already told you how Melody almost single-handedly drove off this Wilson Teager and his crew. She's in Kansas City now, hunting down an Englishman called Born Gallant. Before we were attacked last night she'd ridden to a tumbledown set-tlement called Salvation Creek, and she witnessed something quite extraordinary. Apparently Gallant deliberately challenged Teager and one of his cronies in the saloon, accused him of murder. They were armed, two guns apiece. Gallant finished them both off with his bare hands.'

'Just the one, Jim,' Rebecca called. 'Melody shot the other man dead, here, last night. Before that, she'd helped Gallant escape from the Creek.'

'That's right, she downed an outlaw called Tyne Messner,' Lake said, noting with considerable amuse-ment the wide-eyed surprise – bordering on disbelief – of the other men. 'I know Teager's already proved he's far from finished, but the point I'm making is that if he knows this man Gallant's here, he's surely

102

going to think twice about trying again.'

'Gallant won't be needed,' a laconic voice rasped.

The tall man standing well away from the three ranchers was pared bone and muscle, as lean as a peeled fence pole inside faded clothes and as brown as sun-dried rawhide. He had his back to one of the broken windows. Weather-bleached hair with grey streaking the temples was lifted by the breeze. Grey eyes were enmeshed in nests of fine wrinkles.

'Mack served with the Texas Rangers,' Creed said to Lake. 'Years of experience in range wars, troubles with Apache and Sioux. . . .'

'I'm impressed,' Lake said, unable to keep the scepticism from his voice as he looked across at the lean Texan. 'I'll leave you to tell Melody she's consigned to the kitchen,' he said, 'but while you've still got your teeth you can tell me why we don't need Born Gallant.'

'Because by the time your daughter gets here with the Englishman,' Flynn said, 'you'll be long gone. All three of you.'

'Very sensible,' Lancing said, nodding happily. 'I'm quite sure Kansas City's the best place to be.'

'Wrong. That's the best place to be if you want to die,' Flynn said. 'You're the top men, presidents of two associations hoping to merge. But there'll be scores of men gathering in town for this convention, many of 'em opposed to your ideas. We *know* about Wakeman, Callan and Farrell, that's why we can handle them and their hired guns. Others out there are unknown to you. In Kansas City they'll come at you out of a dark alley, hit you from behind—'

Lancing stopped him with a raised hand. 'So what do you propose?'

'My idea is for somewhere remote, somewhere deep in the wilderness, and I'm thinking of one of the Rocking L's line cabins.'

Lake shook his head. 'Not possible. It's roundup time. The cabins we've got will be in use.'

'All right. Then somewhere between here and town there must be a deserted dwelling, a shack in the woods used but long abandoned, even an empty cave for God's sake.'

Lake was unconvinced, and he could see difficulties Mack Flynn had overlooked.

'What's wrong with right here?'

'Because this is where they expect to find you. Staying here is like nailing a sign to a tree, an arrow pointing the way.'

'If we move out,' Lake said, suddenly angry, 'my wife is left unprotected.'

'Not according to what you've been telling us,' Flynn said, his gaze mocking. 'Won't the gallant Englishman make sure nothing happens to her? With your daughter's help, of course.'

'Isn't that a valid argument against your own idiotic proposal? If Gallant and Melody can defend the property against attackers to protect Rebecca, they can do exactly the same if we're all here – especially when there's a man backing them up who's fought Apaches and Sioux—'

'I think moving out is an excellent idea.' The

tubby rancher, Henry Lancing, was up out of his chair. 'Takes trouble away from the womenfolk, puts the three of us closer to town for when we need to head in for the meeting. If you can come up with a suitable place, Jim, Teager and his men will have no idea where we are and they'll be too short of time to do much chasing around after ghosts.'

'Wakeman, Callan and Farrell are out to stop the merger, stop Consolidated,' Creed pointed out. 'To do that, they must stop us.'

'Ever heard of hostages?' Lake said. 'They could hold a gun to Rebecca's head. That would force my hand. If you think I'd leave my wife with that possibility hanging over her head—'

'Bring her with you.'

'I'm not a sack of clothing, a parcel to be passed around,' Rebecca Lake said.

She was standing in the kitchen doorway, glaring at Flynn.

'Rebecca—'

'No, Jim. I do think it's a good idea for you and your colleagues to move out, but I do *not* intend to go with you; I'll feel quite safe here with Melody and this man she's gone looking for. Now, there was a prospector called Logan who stubbornly panned for gold in a miserable muddy creek some fifteen miles from here. He gave up years ago, just upped sticks and rode away on his bony mule.'

'And his shack's still there, in that rocky hollow.' Lake nodded, feeling slightly sick but knowing he'd lost the argument. 'Yes, I know it. The last time I rode by it still had some of its roof, but there's no glass in the windows—'

'Window,' Rebecca said. 'There's just the one.'

'Yes.' Lake smiled absently. 'The shack's out in the open – but that's good, isn't it? Nobody can approach without being seen. There's a few trees scattered about, there's natural spring water running down to the creek.'

'And the hollow is quite out of the way, remote,' Rebecca said. 'People hereabouts know the story of Logan, the eccentric prospector, but Teager and his men. . . .'

'Texans and outlaws are a long way from home, strangers in a sprawling state as vast as an ocean,' Lake said, nodding as he warmed to the idea. 'They'll *never* find Logan's place.'

'We'll need supplies for at least a day,' Lancing said, thinking ahead, and he glanced enquiringly at Rebecca.

She nodded. 'There's plenty. Your visit's been planned for some time.'

'And now we're leaving you without warning.' Creed smiled apologetically.

'You'll stay for lunch, though, leave early after-noon?'

'That sound reasonable, Mack?' Creed looked at Flynn. 'What about you? Are you coming along with us, or. . . ?'

Flynn shook his head. 'I'm being paid to do a job. Getting you somewhere safe is only part of it. There's still tough opposition out there, and I want to check

106

on this Teager. I hear he's south of here, staying at a spread owned by someone called Taylor.'

'No.' Lake shook his head, frowning a little, wondering where Flynn had got the information. 'Teager's living in a shack in Salvation Creek.'

'Well, that's as maybe,' Flynn said. 'With time running short he's just as likely to be at the Taylor spread with the Texans, discussing tactics. When you move out this afternoon, just point me in the right direction and I'll head off and do some scouting.'

'Look at the man,' Lancing said, grinning, 'he just cannot wait to get back in the saddle, go looking for trouble.'

'Is that it?' Rebecca said, gazing intently at Flynn. 'Are you looking for trouble?'

'If it's out there,' Flynn said, 'I'd like to head it off before it comes looking for us.' He raised an eyebrow, waited to see if she would pursue the subject.

Rebecca smiled. 'All right. I'll scribble directions on a scrap of paper so you can find your way to the prospector's cabin. I take it you will be coming back this way, then riding on to look after your three charges?'

'Oh, I'll look after them, OK,' Flynn said. 'That's the one thing they can count on.'

And there was something in the way he said the words, something in the unspoken message that seemed to pass between Mack Flynn and Rebecca, that caused James Lake to shiver with a sudden and unexpected sense of foreboding.

ELEVEN

'It's too quiet,' Melody said.

'You're used to gunshots, bullets slamming into walls, men howling in pain – yes, I can see how blue skies, balmy air and the sound of birds twittering in the trees would seem strange.'

'Don't be a fool. Look, there's not a sign of life anywhere. If those ranchers from Palo Duro have arrived I should at the very least see a couple of strange horses in the corral. There are none – and, come to that, where's my pa's blue roan?'

'You can't seriously expect me to answer that, can you?'

'Seriously? No. I've only known you for a short time, but I don't expect you to take *anything* seriously.'

She flashed him a quick smile, but it was the first time he had seen a strained look on her face and he knew she was genuinely concerned.

They were riding down the long curve leading to the Rocking L's yard. It was late afternoon. Instead of heading straight for the Lake ranch when they left the café, they'd spent some time in town.

Melody wanted another word with Stick McCrae so she'd ridden over to the *Kansas City Star*'s offices on West 6th Street.

Gallant had drifted along to the Pinkertons' offices in the hope of giving Max Tremblay a heart attack. The fat man with the close-set eyes and thin moustache hadn't turned a hair at sight of him, and that lack of reaction at once set Gallant to thinking. Clearly, word of the happenings at Salvation Creek had got back to the Pinkertons' new manager. Melody Lake had seen off Teager's sidekick, so it looked as if Teager himself had ridden into town after the abortive raid on the Rocking L.

Tremblay might be a slimy character whom William Pinkerton looked on with deep suspicion, but that didn't make him a fool. As he and Melody drew nearer to the Rocking L, Gallant was looking ahead at the ranch house with a good deal of trepidation. What the hell was Tremblay up to now? Or, more to the point, what instructions had been given to him by the group of powerful men out to stop Consolidated?

'Ma's OK,' Melody said suddenly, and her relief was so palpable she seemed visibly to wilt in the saddle.

The front door had opened at their approach. They rode across the yard at a canter, dismounted at the rail, and Melody left Gallant to tie the horses as she ran ahead. When he caught up with her at the front door, she and her mother had embraced, then parted. Rebecca Lake was holding her daughter at arms' length as she watched Gallant approach.

Born Gallant, his senses alert to every nuance in the atmosphere around the Rocking L, saw a woman in her early forties with dark hair flecked with grey and intelligent eyes that, in his opinion, were registering serious concern. That assessment was confirmed when she spoke.

'Come inside, both of you. We've a lot to talk about, and there might not be much time. I think we're knee deep in trouble and, if I'm right, Creed and Lancing brought it with them.'

'I don't trust Mack Flynn,' said Rebecca Lake.

'If he comes recommended by Creed and Lancing, who hired him to ride shotgun,' Gallant said, 'don't you think it would be sensible to abide by their judgement.'

Wrong word, sensible. Using it in that way suggested she wasn't. Gallant winced even as it slipped past his lips. Rebecca's nostrils flared with anger.

'I'm sensible enough to trust my own assessment of character, and Mack Flynn sets warning bells clanging. I've had a good look at him, you haven't. As for judgement, you're a newcomer in a strange land, Mr Gallant. You should spend a few years getting to know the inhabitants before sticking your neck out.'

'Call me Born,' Gallant said automatically. He was standing by the table, arms folded. 'I was merely suggesting no two successful businessmen anywhere in the world would employ a man without checking his credentials.'

'I'm sure they tried their best. But the testimonials to Flynn's supposed qualities take the form of wooden crosses marking men's graves scattered across the West.' She let that sink in, then said, 'After lunch I spoke to Arthur Creed. What he had to say strengthened my suspicions.'

'Before you go on, Ma,' Melody said, 'I now know all about Consolidated, all about Pa's involvement, so I'll know what you're talking about. I got the whole story from Stick McCrae.'

'About time. I always wanted to tell you, especially after last night's bloodshed – but you were gone so quickly.'

'It needed to be done, and it certainly wasn't a wasted trip.' Melody smiled encouragingly. 'Go on, you were saying?'

'Back in Texas it was Mack Flynn who persuaded Creed and Lancing to get on the train and come north a day early. They agreed readily, because it gave them extra time in Kansas City. The convention's being held in the main hotel, everything had been arranged by wire and they wanted to meet the manager, look over the meeting rooms.'

'So far so good,' Gallant said. 'But I must have a devious mind, because I can see what's coming next.'

'Can you?'

'Flynn went missing, didn't he? Pushed off on his own?'

Rebecca smiled wanly. 'I can see why Melody wants

111

you with us. Yes, he did. He walked out of the hotel, and was gone for a long time. When he eventually returned, Creed asked him where he'd been. Flynn smiled in a way that ruled out any more questions – and he made that clear by pointing out that he'd been hired to do a job, and should be left to do it his way.'

'If you're right, and he's not to be trusted,' Gallant said, 'that's an ambiguous remark that takes on sinister undertones. Questions spring to mind. Hired by whom, and what exactly is the job?'

A tense silence settled over the room as the implications of that hung in the air like a menacing storm cloud. Rebecca, unable to keep still, got up from her chair and went to stare out of the shattered window. Melody was sitting in her father's big easy chair, close to his desk. She was leaning back against the colourful old blanket, relaxed but clearly mulling over everything her mother had said, and the import of Gallant's last weighted remark. For the moment, Gallant realized, she seemed to have forgotten what had been troubling her as they rode in to the Rocking L.

'Where is everybody?' he said softly. 'Melody remarked on the silence when we rode in, the absence of horses in the corral, her pa's blue roan.'

'Flynn's idea again,' Rebecca said. 'I went along with it, because I thought it was a good one.' She turned to face them. 'They've all moved to a shack abandoned years ago by a half crazy prospector: Creed, Lancing, my husband, Jim. It's closer to

112

Kansas City, but in a rocky hollow well off the trail. Teager will never find it.'

'You didn't mention Flynn. Didn't he go with them?'

'No. He's gone scouting. He wanted to check on those outlaws, and the Texans who are causing all the trouble.'

'You also said you *thought* it was a good idea. Have you changed your mind?'

Rebecca came away from the window. She sat stiffly in Lake's swivel chair, her elbows on the desk.

'If I'm right to mistrust the man, then I think I've made a terrible mistake.' She picked up a pencil, turned it in her fingers. 'I used this, wrote directions on the back of an envelope so that when he's finished scouting he can find his way directly to the cabin. Nothing elaborate: follow the trail north, swing to the east where a rocky bluff rears up out of the trees and follow the twisting course of a muddy creek. He'll get there.'

'He will – or someone else,' Melody said, her face registering dismay. 'Goodness, I do hope you're wrong about that man.'

But Rebecca was no longer listening. Like Melody and Born Gallant she had caught the sound of hoof-beats coming down the trail and into yard. She swung the chair round to face the window, sprang to her feet, and suddenly her face was flushed with excitement.

'Maybe I have been unfair to him,' she said. 'I thought he was up to Lord knows what kind of

113

underhand business, but that's Flynn riding into the yard now.'

'Not a sign of them,' Flynn said. 'I rode through Salvation Creek and on to the Taylor spread. It's deserted. Corral's empty: no Wakeman, no Farrell, no Callan – no bearded outlaw with battered countenance and an empty holster.' He winked at Gallant. 'I guess you were too much for him, feller. Figured he's not getting paid near enough to risk another beating, or worse. He's turned tail and run, and without him to do their dirty work those Texan ranchers are lost.'

'So where are they?'

'My guess is they're heading for town, Becky—'

'My husband calls me Becky, not you, Flynn.' She smiled sweetly. 'So what are you saying? The outlaws have dispersed. Wakeman and his colleagues had decided to put a brave face on it, turn up at the Kansas City convention and let the merger go ahead unopposed?'

'Oh, I think they'll raise objections. But from what I hear your husband's carrying a briefcase with documentation that plugs every loophole, ties every last knot.'

'Yes,' Rebecca said, 'he's worked long and hard to make sure this merger goes ahead without a hitch.'

Gallant, watching her closely, could tell by the grim set of her face that once again she was not happy. The flush of excitement had given way to the pallor of tension. Her breathing had quickened; she

114

was edgy, clearly uncertain what to do next.

'You're worried those rich ranchers from south of the border haven't given up?' he said, keeping his voice level, matter of fact. 'You think Flynn not seeing them or their hired guns could mean they're on their way to this Logan fellow's cabin?' He smiled and shook his head. 'But you know that's not possible. They know nothing about the cabin. The plan was hatched just a few hours ago, here in this room. Flynn knows, yes, but he's working for Creed and Lancing – and he's still got those directions in his pocket.'

The lean Texan had walked into the room, spurs jingling, and had stood with feet planted as he told his story. Now he dipped a finger into his vest pocket and pulled out the crumpled envelope. He took a couple of long strides and placed it on the corner of the desk. His grey eyes were amused.

'Doesn't take a clever man to figure out he's been the subject of discussion – and come out of it looking bad. Doesn't surprise me in the least, because it's the price I pay for the work I do. But you can quit worrying about my allegiances. Right now, I have none. Ranchers and outlaws have scattered. The job I had is over almost before it had started. There's nothing left for me to do, so I'm going home.'

Without another word he tipped his hat to Rebecca and walked out of the room. They heard his boots clatter on the boards, the jingle of harness; listened with a sense of disbelief as Mack Flynn rode away from the Rocking L.

TWELVE

Arn Wakeman was a rich rancher from northern Texas who looked a man in the eye, talked straight, but wasn't averse to bending the rules to preserve what he called a man's God-given right to freedom. The Consolidated Cattle Growers Association of the United States was an organization that appealed to him about as much as barbed wire had done when it had first been strung between fence posts and begun dividing up the open range. He'd opposed the new fencing at the demonstrations in San Antonio in 1876, and had walked away in fury when the wire with its sharpened spikes was greeted with enthusiasm.

He'd learned from his mistakes, and his opposition to Consolidated had been more organized, and conducted with little concern for scruples. Persuading Mack Flynn to change horses, as it were, had cost money but had been a master stroke. Thanks to the former Texas Ranger, Creed, Lancing and Lake were now isolated, and defenceless.

117

It was late afternoon when Wakeman rode out from old man Taylor's spread, a big man sitting tall in the saddle and with his sharp blue eyes fixed on a distant destination that was out of sight but fixed indelibly in his mind. He had a businessman's brain accustomed to storing masses of facts and figures. Rebecca Lake's written instructions, shown to him by Mack Flynn, had been glanced at once then pushed aside. The cabin that had once been home to a crazy prospector would be easy to find, the rocky hollow one of few in that part of Kansas. When he located it, and the men who had ridden there to hide, the organization called Consolidated would become a nightmare of their lost, broken dreams.

Wakeman was accompanied by Mack Flynn and Wilson Teager. Grant, continually moaning as he nursed his broken wrist, had worn down Hayes and talked him into walking away from the fight. Both men had left at dawn that morning, riding off into the damp mist hanging like smoke in the pine trees. Ten minutes after their dust had settled, Wilson Teager couldn't keep the smug satisfaction from his battered countenance. Wakeman had told him bluntly that, if he stayed loyal for the next couple of days, the bearded outlaw would pocket the pay that had been promised to all four men.

Twenty miles after setting out from the Broken T, Flynn left them to ride on to the Rocking L and spin a tale given at least a grain of truth by the desertion of Grant and Hayes. Wakeman and Teager rode a wide loop that swept them well clear of the Lakes' ranch house. From then on their route took them across Rocking L range, and more than once they had to change direction as in the distance they saw the flapping canvas of a chuck wagon, heard the cries of men and the bawling of cattle and knew that they were crossing the path of the roundup.

The land gradually became more undulating, the ruddy setting sun casting long purple shadows. An hour after Flynn had left them Teager lifted a gloved hand to point ahead to a high bluff of white rock, a few miles beyond that their horses' hoofs were rattling and splashing along the twisting course of a creek in which brown water gurgled over flat stones. Within ten minutes they rode up the bank and through a stand of wilting grey cottonwoods and saw ahead of them a grassy hollow bounded on three sides by steep slopes of rock and scrub. A crumbling log cabin stood close to the creek's muddy waters. A hitch rail stood on bare ground before the door. In the fading evening light, three horses could be seen in deep shadow at the side of the cabin. They were restrained by the ropes of a makeshift corral. Their ears were pricked, their eyes showing white as they looked towards the trees. One of them whickered softly.

'That'll cause those fellers to prick up their ears, spoil their dinner,' Teager said.

'Doesn't help us much,' Wakeman said. 'What little I know of Creed and Lancing doesn't have me quaking in my boots, but James Lake could be trouble.'

Even as he spoke, his horse squealed and reared up on its hind legs as a bullet kicked up dust and rocks. The muzzle flash flared bright red in the cabin's single window. The crack of the rifle echoed flatly from the rocky slopes.

They were out in the open, exposed in the sun's dying rays. There was no cover. It was move fast, or wait for the next bullet to slam into warm living flesh. With a curse, Teager cruelly raked his horse with his spurs and sent it galloping straight towards the cabin. Given no choice, he rode furiously, straight into the eye of the unseen rifle.

Over his shoulder he yelled, 'Round the side's safest.'

From that one window, the rifleman's field of fire was restricted. Wakeman realized that Teager, drawing on experience, had seized on their only chance. Without hesitation he flattened himself along his horse's neck and spurred after the outlaw. In seconds their thundering pace ate up the hundred yards of parched grass. A second shot cracked, but by then they were riding across the face of the cabin and were difficult targets. Wakeman was close enough to be dazzled by the muzzle flash, to taste the gunpowder, to imagine he could feel the heat on his face. Then he leaned back in the saddle, legs braced and reins twisted in his fist as he used his shoulder and thigh muscles to spin the horse around the end of the cabin.

Facing him, holding his skittish mount on a tight rein, Teager was grinning. His teeth were jagged white chips of bone seen through the coarse black hair of his beard. He coughed and spat.

'There's no way out for them, which means we can put that merger on hold without shedding a single drop of blood. 'Stead of filling them full of lead, why don't we sit out here and keep 'em pinned down until that deadline's come and gone?'

'And eat dry grass, drink from that filthy creek, sleep on stony ground?' Wakeman shook his head. 'There's no limit to man's cunning, no saying what they'll try if we give them time. I don't intend to take risks. We finish it now.'

'You got any ideas?'

'Isn't that why you're getting four men's pay?'

'Yeah, you've got one hell of a sweet point there.' Teager thought for a moment, then winked at Wakeman and raised his voice. 'I say we burn them out, Arn. This old cabin'll go up like dry tinder, like to roast 'em alive.'

Wakeman knew Teager was right. It had been a long hot summer. The cabin's walls were of log, the flat roof nothing more than packed brushwood laid across transverse saplings. The fire should be started there. The brushwood would catch instantly, rain flaming brands down on to the cabin's occupants. The three men, burning, choking, would come tumbling out into the open air.

'Get to it,' Wakeman growled.

Dropping the reins, Teager swung a leg down from his horse and began to scout about in the dusk, gathering dry grass and twigs.

Wakeman also dismounted. He eased his rifle from its boot, and stepped forward so he could see around the side of the cabin, keep an eye on the door. He could hear Teager tramping about on the rocky slope behind the cabin, the crackle of scrub, the occasional muttered curse. Then the outlaw reappeared. He was using both hands to bind a bundle of brushwood with tough strands of grass to form a torch.

A sharp noise, the creak of a hinge, snapped Wakeman's head around. A head had poked cautiously out of the cabin's door. It was no more than a dark blob silhouetted against the red night skies, the outline of a Stetson. Smiling thinly, Wakeman jacked a shell into the rifle's breech. At the unmistakable metallic clack the head jerked as if stung. Wakeman saw the pallor of skin as the face turned towards him, the wet shine of light on staring eyes. Casually, he pulled the trigger, fired with the rifle held across his body. The man's hat flew high, spun lazily towards the creek like a leaf caught in the breeze. There was a clatter as he threw himself bodily back into the cabin.

Wakeman turned towards Teager. The outlaw was watching him, his eyes glinting approval.

'Light this for me, Arn. Pretty soon now that feller's going to be sorry he didn't take the bullet.'

'Wait. Go around behind the cabin, cut those ropes, set the horses free.'

Still with his eyes on the cabin's door, Wakeman waited until he heard the sound of horses moving, then watched them appear from the other side of the cabin and toss their heads as they raced down the slope to the creek. Seconds later, Teager was back, brandishing the torch.

Wakeman dug matches out of his vest pocket, moved close to Teager and scraped one alight on the sole of his boot. The outlaw had packed fine, dry grass at the heavy end of the makeshift torch. Wakeman applied the flame. The grass caught at once, crackling as it flared. Teager stepped back. He held the torch down so that the flames rapidly burned upwards. When the torch was blazing he took another step backwards, whirled it once around his head and tossed it up on to the flat roof.

At once, inside the cabin, a man yelled a warning.

Teager drew his six-gun, walked clear of the cabin and a few yards down the slope towards the creek. Then he turned to face the door.

Wakeman followed slowly. Already the brushwood roof was alight. The cabin's door was ill-fitting, and through that and the glassless window a fierce draught was feeding the fire. Brilliant tongues of flame shot high above the cabin, licking the air, lighting the hollow's rocky walls, casting flickering shadows across the grass and turning the creek's muddy waters into rivers of gold. Sparks flew like dancing fireflies, and over and above the brilliance of the show there was a menacing hissing and an ever increasing roar as the fire took hold.

A muted snapping and crackling and cries of fear or pain told Wakeman that the blazing roof was collapsing into the cabin's single room. Suddenly the door was flung open. Beyond it no darkness was visible; the room seemed to be a boiling mass of flame in which no human could stay alive. Out of that raging inferno stumbled a man Wakeman didn't recognize. He was coughing, choking, slapping at his clothes. With one hand he was clinging to a heavy briefcase. He staggered a few yards away from the cabin, tripped, went down on his knees in the grass. Through streaming eyes he stared wildly at Wilson Teager.

Teager lifted his heavy Peacemaker, and pulled the trigger.

The shot was a vicious crack slicing though the roar of the fire. The kneeling man reared up and backwards, mouth open. The briefcase fell from his hand. He clutched at his shoulder. Through his clawing fingers, in the light of the fire, blood shone wetly.

Then, as Wakeman watched dispassionately, almost without interest, Creed and Lancing came tumbling from the blazing shack. Creed's hair was on fire, his clothes smouldering. He used his hat to slap frantically at his head, then threw himself to the ground and rolled on the night-damp grass. Lancing's face was blackened. He was struggling to breathe. He stopped and bent over, bracing himself with his hands on his knees. He sucked at the air with painful, rasping gasps.

Again Teager lifted his Peacemaker. He snicked back the hammer, levelled the big six-gun at Lancing.

'No,' Wakeman called sharply above the roar of the flames. 'Let them live. I've got a better idea.'

'I had a better idea,' Teager said, not lowering the gun but allowing the barrel to tilt upwards. 'You didn't like it.'

'And I don't like murder, though it attracts because death is permanent. However, what I'm proposing now will stop Consolidated in its tracks,' Wakeman said, 'and it's so damn simple I can't believe I didn't think of it before now.'

THIRTEEN

The sharp tang of woodsmoke came strong enough on the night air to sting their eyes when, according to Melody Lake, they were still a mile away from Logan's cabin. Even as the pungent aroma reached them Born Gallant was flinging an arm high to point to a faint glow that could be seen reflecting from low clouds above the tops of trees that were but dark irregular shapes atop a bluff that loomed a ghostly white.

At once he was left standing as Melody lightly touched her buckskin with blunt spurs and the nimble beast eagerly spurted from a canter to a furious gallop in the space of several raking strides.

Over the next few frantic minutes that furious ride reminded Gallant strongly of the flight from Salvation Creek when the girl with the lustrous flowing hair had laughed gaily as she rode away from him across the Kansas prairie. Then they had been fleeing from men with guns. Now they were . . . what? Gallant wasn't quite sure what to expect but,

126

knowing that up ahead lay an old log cabin in which three businessmen men who were no longer young were hiding from opponents out to stop their grand, far-sighted plans at all costs, it wasn't difficult to make an educated guess.

The best he could hope for, if he was right and it was the cabin that was on fire, was that all three men had got clear. But Gallant had served with armies in many trouble spots on the Asian sub-continent, and his experiences in savage battles had taught him that fires were always set for a purpose. If that purpose was not to trap people in a blazing inferno, then it was to drive them out into the open – with clear and brutal consequences.

He had fallen fifty yards behind Melody when the drumming of her horse's hoofs on hard earth changed to the hard rattle of metal on stone. As he swung after her he saw that she was following the course of a small creek. Water splashed high, glittering as it caught the light. Then, dramatically, those splashes changed colour and, as they surged on through a thin grove of cottonwoods, Gallant saw that they had reached a hollow that was suffused with light as if lit by the setting sun.

He was closing on her as she rode away from the creek and across a grassy slope, and he knew that she had instinctively slowed, petrified at what she might find. But to Gallant, clear headed, less personally involved, all was instantly clear. Set against rocky slopes, the cabin was already nothing more than a collapsed ruin of smouldering logs and fiercely glowing embers. And in front of it, clearly visible, three men could be seen in various attitudes. The tension in their poses was palpable. They had escaped from the blazing cabin, but at what cost? For on night air warmed by a fire that had consumed a log dwelling that had withstood the ravages of the years, Gallant could also detect the lingering tang of gunsmoke.

'A flesh wound, that's all it is,' James Lake said thickly. 'I'm OK, I'll live.'

His voice was hoarse from the smoke. He was sitting with his back against one the hitch rail's uprights. His upper body was naked, and the remains of his shirt was being fashioned into a crude sling for his left arm by Arthur Creed.

James Lake had suffered a gunshot wound. Creed and Henry Lancing were uninjured, but badly shaken. They had escaped from the blazing cabin after Lake. They'd heard the gunshot above the roar of the flames and seen Lake on the ground clutching his shoulder. With flames licking at their backs, singeing their clothing and searing their flesh, they'd gritted their teeth and leaped through the doorway to face the unseen gunman. Instead of being met by a blast of hot lead from the outlaw's Peacemaker, they'd heard Arn Wakeman telling him to let them live.

'And that,' Creed had told Gallant, 'hit us almost as hard as a bullet. When a man's been bracing himself to face death, something like that comes as an awful anticlimax,' he had said, a wry grin creasing his scorched face.

'After seeing that fire from a distance,' Gallant said, 'finding the three of you alive came as a shock to me, too. You say Teager was told to hold his fire – if it was Teager.'

'Oh yes, it was Wilson Teager with Wakeman,' Lake said. 'Teager was the one who plugged me when I half fell out of the door. You've encountered him in Salvation Creek, haven't you? You know he's a brutal man?'

'We look on each other,' Gallant said drily, 'with considerable respect – but, do go on.'

'If it had been up to Teager,' Creed said, roughly knotting the sling behind Lake's elbow and using the rail to help him climb to his feet, 'he would have waited for us to come running out of that burning cabin, then finished the job with three well-placed bullets not just the one that winged Jim. Indeed, from the fierce argument that raged between the two of them, those were his instructions he was determined to follow.'

Melody frowned. 'What . . . and Wakeman changed his mind and called him off?'

'Came up with a better idea,' Lancing said. 'Of course, Teager didn't like it. He likes the finality of a bullet. No way back from that.'

'So they argued,' Gallant said, 'but Wakeman won and you all escaped death because he found another way of stopping this Consolidated malarkey.'

'Simple, foolproof, didn't require the discharge of

a single weapon,' James Lake said bitterly. 'He took the briefcase.'

Gallant heard Melody gasp, saw her hand go to her mouth, saw her swing away to stare down at the creek.

'My daughter grasps the significance at once,' Lake said. 'That's because she understands law, and knows exactly what we need to carry this merger through. The three of us here must have with us, when we walk into that conference room, official papers that have been signed, sealed, stamped and authenticated – and everything we need is in that worn leather holdall. Every legal document, every bank statement, every cattle manifest, the minutes of every meeting at which important motions were carried, the name of every man or organization backing us with their power and their money – everything.'

'And where is it now? Where's he taken it?'

Melody's hair swirled about her shoulders, shining like ebony in the glow of the dying fire as she spun to face her father. The shock that had forced her to turn away had been brushed off effortlessly, as if it had been nothing more than the fleeting touch of a moth's wings. Her face now was not pale, but glowing, her eyes alight. Her hands were planted on her hips as she asked the question, her chin thrust determinedly, and every man there understood from the slight curl to her full lips and the expectant look on her face as she waited that she already knew the answer.

But what she wanted – and this they also understood – was more understanding from her father, and his acceptance, however reluctant given, that their last chance to save Consolidated lay with his daughter and the enigmatic Englishman called Born Gallant.

For some moments all that could be heard was soft breathing, the crackle and hiss of the dying embers, the distant gurgle of the creek's tumbling waters.

'All right, my dear,' James Lake said at last, and he smiled wearily. 'You were right when Teager raided the Rocking L, you were right when you rode into Kansas City to ask a journalist to lead you to . . . to this man' – he gestured, not unkindly, to Born Gallant – 'and you were right not to trust me to look after myself—'

'Nonsense. People have their own particular, special strengths,' Melody said. 'Yours has been playing a major part in the realization of a cattle-man's dream.'

'Now shattered.'

'No.' Melody shook her head. 'Because although I will one day be an excellent lawyer, I have certain unusual strengths that are shared by the man I rode to Kansas City to find, the man I brought back with me.'

Lake nodded. 'I know. I've just said that I recognize what you have done already. If you think you can get those documents back from Wakeman, well. . . .' He took a deep breath. 'I'd like you to try, yet I'm frightened to say it because more than anything I want you to take care, to. . . .'

His words faltered. Unable to continue, he shook his head helplessly.

'The strengths I share with Gallant,' Melody said softly, 'will be more than enough to overcome businessmen like Arn Wakeman, who is a selfish, shallow individual without imagination or vision, and men like Wilson Teager and his outlaw cronies who are all cowards—'

'Mack Flynn, too,' interrupted Born Gallant, 'for clearly that mean-looking ranger had a hand in this.'

'Mack?' Creed was astounded. 'But he's working for us.'

'Maybe he is,' Melody said, 'but he's also drawing wages from the other side. Getting word from Flynn is the only way Wakeman and Teager could have found out about this place.' She shook her head irritably, and frowned at Gallant. 'Anyway, Flynn's gone, he's out of it, you were there and you heard what he said and saw him leave.'

'Of course I did,' Born Gallant said with a grin. 'But despite what Mr Flynn would like us to believe, what we don't know is where he's gone, or what he's up to now.'

FOURTEEN

Arn Wakeman's bold theft of the briefcase and the vital documents it contained had taken the heat off the two presidents, Creed and Lancing, and James Lake; with Consolidated dead on the ground, the three men were no longer in danger.

After sluicing their sore, blackened faces in the icy waters of the creek, Creed and Lancing had collected their horses from the cottonwoods where they had wandered after being chased off by Teager, and had set out for Kansas City and the comfort of a big hotel.

Gallant helped Lake up on to his horse, and Melody pressed her buckskin close to her father's blue roan during the ride to Rocking L that was made mostly in silence. Lake was white with pain, a stiff figure in the saddle with his good hand holding tight to the horn. Melody called occasional short halts to let her father rest and slake his raging thirst with the tepid water in her canteen, but for the most part she too was lost in thought.

When they reached the ranch house, light was flooding from the open door. Rebecca had picked up

the sounds of their approach, and was waiting anx-
iously. Gallant helped Lake down from his horse and
into the house while Melody gave her mother a quick
run down on all that had happened.

Five minutes after riding into the yard, Gallant
and Melody were back in the saddle and on their way
south to the Taylor spread.

'Our main problem,' Gallant said, 'is we don't know
what we're up against. Three men for sure, that's the
ranchers from Texas – Wakeman, Callan and Farrell
– and the callous disregard for human life when they
attacked the cabin proves that Wakeman's at least as
dangerous as Teager. He'll be there, and the other
man whose wrist your ma snapped, then Hayes—'

'And Mack Flynn, if you're right and he was lying
to us.'

They had ridden a half circle to avoid the settlement of Salvation Creek, pushed on in a southerly
direction and were now reined back in the trees
above the Broken T. A wind had picked up, and
branches above their heads were clattering, dead
leaves skittering along the trail. A pale moon was
lighting the yard, the windmill, the rotten fence, the
single storey house. Inside, just one oil lamp was lit.
By its light a man could be seen in one of the big
chairs, sitting smoking. Hanging on the back of the
chair was a gunbelt, brass shells glinting in its loops.

'Oh, he was lying all right,' Gallant said, 'yet even
if I got that right I could still be talking through my
hat. At this time of night we'd naturally expect men

134

to be in bed, yet the quiet down there is still discon-
certing. And I don't know about you, but from here
I can see just three horses in that corral.'

'Dammit,' Melody said softly, 'then where the hell
is everybody?'

'Not needed now Wakeman's taken matters into
his own hands?' Gallant suggested.

'Well, Creed and Lancing figure it's all over, the
danger past, that's why they've ridden on to town.
Pa's hurt, despondent, and he can't see how we can
pull this off with time slipping away like sand out of
a holed bucket.' She nodded. 'You're probably right.
If Wakeman believes he's in control of the situation,
he's bound to be confident enough to dismiss the
hired help.'

Gallant pulled thoughtfully at his lip.

'Even if the gunslingers have been paid off and
Mack Flynn really was heading home,' he said, 'that
still leaves three men waiting for us inside that house.
All right, Wakeman's ruthless streak is the exception;
they're wealthy ranchers accustomed to the easy life
and unlikely to cause us much trouble. But there's
another worry. If you think about it, they're losing
sleep guarding a briefcase that doesn't need guarding. A single match would put those papers out of
reach for ever, reduce months of work to ash a light
breeze would turn to dust.'

'Oh, my goodness, Born, don't say that.'

'It's something we've got to bear in mind. It was
Wakeman's idea to seize those papers. If we go burst-
ing in through the front door brandishing guns, that

bright idea just might come to him out of the blue and see him reaching for the matches.'

'So a frontal assault is ruled out?'

He grinned. 'Is that the military term for what I just said?'

'There's a military term for what I'll do to you if you don't shut up and put your mind to this problem.'

'Ma'am, I'm just a common English foot soldier bowing to the superior intelligence of a beautiful young lawyer—'

She leaned across and whacked him over the back of the head with her glove. Both horses started at the sudden movement and sound, rounded, tossed their heads. Brush crackled like distant small arms fire under their trampling hoofs. With a quick jerk on the reins Melody halted her horse's fidgeting, glanced nervously down at the house. Born had swiftly settled his mount and was leaning with his forearms on the horn, grinning.

'We could always burn them out,' he said, 'but that—'

'Would also endanger the papers.' She nodded impatiently, eyes narrowed in thought. 'How does this sound? A timid approach from the front by a young lady here without her father's knowledge, throwing herself on the mercy of ruthless business-men she's sure must have hearts of gold. . . .'

'Is there a back way in?'

'There's a door leading in off a small gallery with a shaky old roof. I visited a couple of times with my mother when I was a child. Taylor's wife was alive, she let me play there with some old wooden toys.'

'If you knock on the front door, raise your voice and look wild-eyed and hysterical when they laugh in your face, you'll hold their attention long enough for me to find a way in.'

'And then. . . ?'

'Depends on the way it unfolds. Looks like two of 'em are in bed. I think that's Wakeman sitting there smoking. Make sure he sees you ride up. He won't be the least bit concerned, you're a young woman, he'll figure he can deal with you on his own without disturbing the others.'

'What if Teager's told him the way I held off gunmen at Salvation Creek.'

'No man alive would believe that unless he saw it with his own eyes.'

'He will do, soon enough,' Melody said emphatically. 'I'll keep him talking as long as I can. When you force that door and get inside, do something to attract his attention – smash a plate in the kitchen, fire a shot through the ceiling. The second he takes his eyes off me, it's all over for him.'

They checked their weapons. Melody had a .44 Remington and her Winchester; Gallant was still carrying Teager's Peacemaker tucked into his waistband. When they were satisfied, they wished each other luck. Their eyes met. Gallant's grin was deliberately devil-may-care. Her answering crooked smile revealed little, but her dark eyes were steady and held not a hint of fear. Enormously impressed by her steely calm, he let his mount drift alongside her buckskin, reached across and touched her cheek very lightly with his knuckles, then moved off.

He had to go the long way round, keeping out of the splashes of moonlight and always on the far side of what trees he could find as he cut a wide circle to the east of the Broken T to ride in across the bare ground on the far side of the corral. The three horses watched his approach, snorting softly. There were no windows on that side of the house. Deliberately he rode through the patch of bright moonlight they had seen from the ridge, and watched as Melody emerged at once from the trees, lifted a hand and started down the trail towards the yard at a noisy canter.

The rear of the house was as she'd described it, but close to derelict from neglect and the erosion of many severe winters. The windows were filthy, draped with curtains that were limp rags, most of the glass broken. The gallery was sagging. Time had reduced the cover Melody remembered to a couple of uprights leaning drunkenly.

Gallant slipped lightly from the saddle, let the reins trail to hold the horse and cat-footed his way towards the house. The damp long grass swished against his boots. A moth fluttered against his mouth, and was gone. When he reached the gallery's boards, moonlight glistening in their slick damp surface, he stopped without climbing up, stood still in the shadows and breathed silently through parted lips.

He could hear Melody's pony stepping lightly across the yard. In his mind he followed its progress.

138

When the sound of movement ceased he pictured the bold young woman dismounting. He let a faint smile touch his lips when the bridle jingled musically and boots scraped on the ground to confirm the picture. Then in an instant he became sober and alert as a heavy thud, and the gruff tones of a man demanding to know what the hell was going on, told him that Arn Wakeman had opened the door.

So much, Gallant thought, *for the big rancher not wanting to disturb his sleeping partners.*

With a quickening of the pulse he stepped up on to the gallery. A rotten board crumbled, as friable as dry mud under his foot. He grabbed for an upright, almost followed it down as it began to lean away from him. Steady again, on firmer footing, he held back a moment longer. Absolutely still. Listening.

Melody and Wakeman were talking. On the whisper of a breeze the sound carried as a droning mumble over the low roof, swelling and receding, words lost. But there was another sound, closer, from inside the house. A creak of boards, or hinges. A hesitant footstep.

Then a match was struck. Yellow light flared – went out.

Grimacing, Gallant stepped gingerly across the uneven boards. One tilted underfoot. A rusty nail squealed like a startled bird. He felt his jaw muscles bulge. In the window's remaining glass his reflection was misshapen, bulking dark against the moonlight trees. If he could see it, so could the other men in the house, those Wakeman had roused from slumber.

But that disturbance would be pulling them in the other direction. They'd be listening to the talk, moving cautiously towards the front door.

Swiftly, Gallant covered the remaining distance across the small gallery and flattened himself against the wall.

The door was flimsy, the handle rusty iron. He reached for it, touched it, tested it without force – and the door swung inwards.

Like a cold shadow carried by the draught, Gallant stepped over the threshold. As he pushed the door to behind him and pressed back against it he caught the smell of the struck match, the dead match, the raw smell of sweat. Then, on the air, he sensed movement, the warmth of a body.

Absolutely still, flat against the flimsy woodwork, he felt his hair prickling. His eyes were wide, straining to adjust to the darkness.

Then there was the sound of a gun being cocked. Gallant shut his eyes.

'Who's there?'

'Flynn.'

Gallant's response was instant, the name intended to confuse, to buy valuable seconds. He grinned, enjoying the shocked silence that was like a bottomless well against the dull mumble of words from the front of the house, the softer pitch of Melody's voice.

The unseen man with the gun seemed dumbfounded.

'Flynn? Aren't you supposed to be—?'

'Change of plan,' Gallant said.

140

And without a sound he slid down the door, took his weight on one hand and stretched his legs out sideways.

'Change of . . . no, wait, there's something wrong, you're not—'

Pivoting on his left hand, Gallant swung his legs across the floor and swept the unseen man's feet from under him. He yelled, fell like a log and hit the floor with a crash. Gallant heard his teeth snapped shut. Simultaneously there was a bang and a brilliant flash as the pistol slammed against the floor and the hammer dropped.

Blinded, blinking away vivid red blotches, Gallant rolled and sprang to his feet. His right hand swept the Peacemaker from his waistband. He could hear the downed man grunting as he struggled to rise. From another part of the house a man was demanding fearfully to know what was happening. Doors banged. Then suddenly Gallant was able to see. An oil lamp was being carried through from the front of the house. It was held high by a big man – Arn Wakeman. The light flashed from wall to wall. He walked along the passage towards Gallant.

Behind him came Melody Lake. She was a gamin figure. Hair swirling, she moved with the grace of a dancer on silent pumps. She looked past Wakeman, at a glance took in the bare kitchen, the man struggling to rise, the cocked Peacemaker. Her eyes met Gallant's. She nodded, took her lip between her teeth.

From her belt, with great care, she drew her .44 Remington and levelled it at Wakeman's broad back.

FIFTEEN

As they'd suspected, sight of a girl approaching the house had intrigued Arn Wakeman but had given rise to no suspicions, had aroused in him no sense of foreboding. He'd gone to the door in a confident mood, the look of pleading on Melody's innocent young face as she poured out her heart had amused him but rung no warning bells – and that had been his undoing.

He had heard the sudden commotion from the rear of the house, the sharp detonation as the six-gun went off, and had rushed to investigate what he believed to be a separate incident. Now, caught between Gallant and Melody Lake in the house's inner passage, he was restricted by the walls and the oil lamp he held in one hand, and was fifteen feet from his gunbelt which was still hanging from the back of the chair in the living room.

'You,' Gallant said, standing by the back door and waggling the Peacemaker at the man on the floor who had a bloody nose and one eye reddened and closing, 'scuttle across the floor on your backside until you're sitting against the wall.'

'Who the hell—'

'Do it.'

'You must be Born Gallant,' the man said, nodding.

He looked down contemplatively at his six-gun. It had fired, punched a hole in the ceiling, but had never left his hand. A drop of blood dripped from his nose, spattered the cylinder. He looked up at Gallant. He seemed to be calculating the odds.

Another man dressed in tight-fitting woollen underwear had poked his head out of one of the bedrooms and was standing in the opening, watching. A six-gun dangled from his hand. He looked amused.

'Benny Callan's stubborn, he won't scuttle anywhere,' he said. 'So am I, as it happens, and you won't shift Arn Wakeman.'

'Looks like there's enough of us here of a similar disposition to form a club,' Gallant said. 'But that's what this is about, isn't it? That's why we've come calling on you. Cattlemen want to form a club, and you're in the way.'

'You've wasted your time,' Wakeman said.

'Don't often do that,' Gallant said. 'Don't intend to do it now, so if you'd kindly fetch the briefcase you took from James Lake—'

'He denies all knowledge of it,' Melody said.

Her voice dripped with sarcasm. Wakeman swung around. Melody smiled sweetly, lifted the Remington in both hands and pointed it at the bridge of his nose.

143

'No.' Wakeman shook his head. 'You're mistaken, my dear. I know all about that leather bag and its contents. What I told you was, I haven't got it.'

The Remington's hammer went back with an ugly snap.

'And now you're mistaken, because we know you've got it,' Melody said. 'You took it from my father, when he was on the ground, bleeding, and now you're going to get it.'

'It happened exactly as you describe it,' Wakeman said, 'but still you are mistaken. You *don't* know I've got it. What you do know is that I had it when I left the burning cabin.'

'Well now,' Gallant said softly. 'I was beginning to suspect something was up. Teager, for a start. Where's he? And his owlhoot pals? And Mack Flynn, the turncoat?' He flicked a glance from Callan to the man in underwear, who had to be Farrell. 'Then there's you two heroes, six-guns in your hands, knowing that if it comes to a fight I can get but one of you, knowing Melody's blocked by Wakeman, yet you're happy to chew the fat.'

'I think we should retire to the dubious comfort of the front room,' Wakeman said, 'and talk this over.'

'You're just not listening, are you?' Gallant said. 'We're talking now and it's getting us nowhere – yet you want to draw it out. That's not going to happen. Callan and Farrell are going to hand their weapons to me, now. Then you three are going to walk down the passage to the front room. The young lady with the steady hands walks backwards ahead of you, makes sure there's no funny business, gets there first. That takes care of Wakeman's six-shooter. Once you're settled, stay settled: she'll shoot the first man to make a move without raising his hand and asking permission.'

'Which leaves you at a loose end,' Wakeman said.

'Wouldn't call it that,' Gallant said. 'I'm going to tear this place apart, room by room, just in case you're trying to pull a fast one and that briefcase is actually here, tucked away under a mattress.'

'I repeat, you're wasting your time,' Wakeman said.

Gallant shook his head. 'Told you, I rarely do that. What I am doing is putting my faith in someone I can trust.' He grinned, stabbed a thumb at his chest. 'That person's yours truly. And when I've finished searching, one way or another I'll know where that briefcase is.'

SIXTEEN

'To find where Teager's staying in Salvation Creek we could climb that hill on foot and knock on doors, rouse people from sleep, ask questions,' Melody said. 'But that will take time. We know we're unlikely to get the right house first time, and by moving through the village we'll be creating a disturbance. Wherever those outlaws are hiding out, they'll hear us coming. That raises the possibility of their resorting to that bright idea you mentioned.'

'Should have asked Wakeman,' Gallant said, 'but in truth I really don't think burning the papers occurred to him. If it didn't cross his mind, Teager certainly won't think of it. If he does think of it, he won't strike the match that turns those papers to blackened flakes, because he hasn't got the authority and it would risk incurring Wakeman's wrath.'

'And kissing his money goodbye. All right, so wherever the papers are, they're safe. What about knocking on doors? Do we risk that?'

'Don't have to,' Gallant said, and he grinned

across at her in the darkness. 'There's no mystery, I know where we'll find Teager.'

'Ah, yes,' Melody said after a moment's thought. 'He'll be in Sundown Tancred's Last Chance saloon, won't he? You'll like that, Gallant. It'll be like returning to a battle ground where distant trumpets evoke haunting memories of recent triumphs.'

'Knew a woman like you in England,' he mused, 'every time she opened her mouth she spouted poetry.'

They'd covered ten miles since leaving the Broken T, first in bright moonlight, then in darkness, as masses of black cloud floated across the moon and shadow covered the Kansas plains like a heavy blanket. With that ten miles added to the ground they'd already covered during the day, their horses were beginning to tire. The time to saddle replacements had been when they dropped James Lake at the Rocking L. It had occurred to both of them but, because of the roundup, there were no suitable mounts available.

At the Broken T, with Wakeman, Callan and Farrell held in the front room by Melody and her .44 Remington, Gallant had set about searching a house in which there were few hiding places. Yet even as he moved from room to room, Wakeman's words were echoing in his ears and he knew he would find nothing. He and Melody had worried about the Texan rancher burning the papers as a permanent solution. Rather than do that he had simply done the obvious, and got rid of them. Given them to Teager.

Sent the bearded bandit back to his hovel.

At no time had he admitted as much, but to Gallant the words he had spoken had been clear enough: 'You're wasting your time'. The amused unconcern that had met them when they broke into the Taylor spread came from supreme confidence. The merger that would lead to the formation of the Consolidated Cattle Growers Association of the United States was like a train that had hit the buffers: the papers were in Salvation Creek; without those papers, the merger was going nowhere.

'We'll see about that,' Gallant mumbled.

Metal tinkled and leather squeaked as Melody twisted in the saddle to stare at him.

'See about what?'

He grinned. 'Thinking aloud. I was having an argument with Arn Wakeman and my back teeth.'

'We're almost back to Salvation Creek. Time would be better spent figuring out how we're going to fight this battle.'

'You're right. Two of us, up against four men—'

'No. Wakeman and the others were talking while you searched Taylor's place. Flynn was right, Hayes and Grant have gone.'

'So it's just Teager and Flynn.'

'Unless Sundown Tancred decides to take sides.'

'Now that would be a sight to see,' Gallant marvelled.

They came off the open grassland and the ground began to slope downwards. As they threaded their way through a shallow arroyo, ahead of them, dark even against the lowering skies, they could see the ugly shapes of Salvation Creek's timber shacks. They were like uneven wooden blocks, piled one on top of the other all the way up the hillside. Lower down, a solitary light glimmered: the Last Chance saloon. The rank smell of the creek was in their nostrils. Bull frogs croaked, but the overall silence was of a kind that sets the nerves on edge.

As if its oppressive weight was becoming too much for her, Melody abruptly swung her pony off the trail and drew rein. When Gallant pulled alongside she was a slim shape in the saddle, very still. What he could see of her face in the night's deep gloom was without expression. She was staring fixedly towards the jumble of black shapes sprawled across the barren hillside.

'I've been talking tough,' she said, turning to him, 'but the closer we get to that fearful place, the more my skin begins to prickle and the more I feel that I'm riding my luck.' Light sparked in her eyes as she looked at him; he wondered if it was the glint of tears. 'It's all very well shooting at men from a distance with a rifle – as I did here to help you escape. And it was quite fun taking pot shots at outlaws attacking my home – though killing a man was sickening, and I don't want to do that again. And there's the problem, isn't it?'

'One of them,' he agreed. 'Discharging a pistol towards flesh and blood of any kind is never to be taken lightly. Death is always waiting to pounce. And of course, the other problem – much worse in my view – is that if we push ahead with this, you're going to be walking boldly into a barroom where dangerous armed men are waiting. That's a lot different from engaging with them from a respectable distance. A lot more personal. And, close up, they look a damn sight more fearsome. The mere sight of certain fellows can set the nerves twanging.'

'But there's no way out of it – not if I'm to get those papers back for my pa.'

'We. If *we're* to get them back; you know you're not alone. In fact,' Gallant said, 'the gent in me is insisting you shouldn't be here at all. Knowing you were riding down the slope to confront old Arn Wakeman didn't upset me at all, which doesn't say a lot for my gallantry, but I'm glad you've brought this out into the open while we've still got time.'

'But that's just it, we haven't got time,' she said. 'You know there's a deadline—'

'Actually, I meant while there's still time to see common sense, Melody, and keep you well clear of that hellhole.'

'Oh, come on, Gallant, you're—'

'I mean it. Look, you were never going to be first man into that saloon, and if you follow me in you might as well not be there. Either they'll be dead, or I will—'

'No, you're not thinking straight.' She shook her head firmly. 'This is not you going up against a gunslinger to see who's top dog. Wilson Teager's got something we want – that briefcase – but you can bet your life that by now it's tucked away in some rat-infested shack on those slopes. Teager doesn't have to do anything. He can sit there and drink the night away. We're not going to walk into the Last Chance and be met by a hail of bullets.'

'Mm, I see what you mean. Being of limited intelligence, he'll believe that if he keeps his mouth shut, I'll go away.' He grinned. 'After what happened to him the last time we met, he's probably praying he's right.'

She chuckled throatily. 'You realize what I'm doing, don't you? I'm convincing myself – and you, of course – that's it's quite safe for me to walk in there with you because he doesn't pose a threat.'

'What happened to the skin prickles, the sickening thought of killing a man?'

'Just proves you can talk yourself out of anything,' she said, flicking the reins and moving back on to the trail. 'Or into it, of course.'

'Funny you should say that,' Gallant said, tucking in behind her pony, 'because that's exactly what we're going to have to do with Teager.'

SEVENTEEN

A single oil lamp hung over the bar, the glass coated with greasy soot.

Underneath it lay the briefcase, on its side, looking tired in the feeble light. Its old, worn leather was scuffed, collapsing in on itself but given solid rectangular form by the bulk of the papers it contained.

Compared to the surroundings, it could have been brand new.

The bar had sagged further since Gallant first saw it. One thick plank was broken – probably stamped on by a horse. Most of the bottles had fallen over, some had rolled to the floor, some had shattered. Over the end of the bar, a cowboy or travelling drummer had put a foot through the floor above. Fragments of timber and old lace hung perilously through the jagged hole, like the contents of an upended broken coffin.

Because of the hour, just two men were in the room. Sundown Tancred was slouched on a stool behind the bar, almost lost in the gloom but looming fully as large as a normal man standing. The heavy plaits were like twisted ropes across his enormous shoulders, the rags tying their ends stained with drink and grease.

Across the worn planks littered with bottles and cigarette butts, standing hip-shot against the timber, was Wilson Teager. He was a pace or two away from the briefcase, as if the item he was guarding had slipped from his mind, or been driven out by the liquor he had consumed. His head was turned towards Gallant. He'd caught the stiff swish of the greasy curtain as Gallant came in out of the night, had perhaps felt the cool draught or been alerted by the watchful 'breed. Even from across the room, in semi-darkness, Teager's eyes gleamed red, shot with blood from the strong drink.

The glass in his hand, Gallant thought wryly, was not his first, not his tenth – but it could so easily be his last. . . .

'You slipped up, Teager,' he said, advancing through the shadows. 'Wakeman won't be pleased. 'Stead of taking that briefcase to your hovel and clutching it in your hot hand you stopped off here to wet your whistle. Now it's too late.'

He stopped four feet from the outlaw, eight from the briefcase.

'Wakeman said he wanted it safe,' Teager growled, and he patted the Peacemaker in its holster on his heavy thigh. 'With me it's as safe as it'll ever be.'

'Which is not very,' Gallant said mildly. 'Where's Flynn?'

'Never heard of him.'

'That's strange. Besides, I thought I heard a horse-man behind me when I rode in. Would that have been him?'

'More likely the girl,' Teager said, and revealed his shattered teeth in a sneering grin. 'Without her to hold your hand, you're nothing.'

'Who's holding yours, now Tyne Messner's gone? Indian Joe over there?'

Behind the bar Tancred stirred his bulk, growled wetly and spat between his feet.

Gallant grinned. 'You should get that throat seen to.'

Teager tossed back his drink and slammed the glass on the bar. It shuddered. Another bottle toppled, rolled. Before the glass in Teager's fist had finished its downward curve, before the falling bottle had hit the sawdust with a dull thud, Gallant had skipped lightly around the outlaw and clamped his hand on the briefcase's grip.

Teager spun to face him, a big man light on his feet. He stared, took in Gallant's casual stance, looked him up and down and shook his head.

'Last time you were here I left my Peacemaker in your keeping. You should have brought it with you, but I don't see it.'

'What the eye doesn't see . . .' Gallant said.

'Unarmed, you'll never make it to the door.'

'Actually, it's a curtain,' Gallant said, 'and I'm about to make the attempt.'

With a jerk, he dragged the old briefcase off the

rough planks. It was in his left hand. It swung, thumped heavily against his knee. Seeming scarcely to be aware of Teager, his eyes on the curtained doorway, he took a step away from the bar, then another, walking as if he had all the time in the world.

Teager's bloodshot eyes widened. His lips parted, formed an ugly wet slit in the black tangle of hair.

Then his whole body coiled. His big hand formed a claw, shot downwards to his thigh. His fingers curled around the butt of the Peacemaker. The gun began to lift, to clear the holster.

Almost lazily, but with speed that was deceptive enough to fool the eye, Born Gallant slipped the Peacemaker out of his waistband and shot the big outlaw between the eyes. The high shot carried the weight of a pile driver. Teager went down as if punched backwards over a waist-high fence. His left arm swept along the bar. Bottles fell, shattering.

'Another lucky shot,' Gallant said, for Tancred's benefit. 'And I hope you employ a cleaning lady.'

The 'breed came off his stool like a dirt shelf detaching itself from a cliff. He scooped up a heavy barrel in both huge hands and it hurled over the bar at Gallant. Without waiting to see the result he followed it, demolishing the bar with a crash of splintering timber as he threw himself at Gallant.

The barrel hit Gallant on his shoulder, continued on its way and smashed a table and chair into matchwood. Gallant staggered sideways. His shoulder and arm went numb. The briefcase fell to the floor. Eyes screwed up in agony he snapped a shot with the Peacemaker even as the reeking 'breed's huge body hit him with the weight of a longhorn steer. Gallant saw Tancred's apron pucker as his shot drilled into the 'breed's ribs. Then he was down on his back in the sawdust with the weight of Tancred's solid flesh bearing down on his face.

Wriggling sideways like a sidewinder snake, Gallant squirmed from under the big saloonist. On his face he felt the warm wetness of blood. He tried to rise. His left arm buckled under him. Then Tancred's arm came over to deliver a mighty blow as he rolled at Gallant. It slammed across Gallant's chest with the weight of a falling tree. Gallant grunted with the shock, lashed out with the Peacemaker. The sight raked down Tancred's face, ripping the skin. The 'breed's plaits whipped as he jerked his head back. He threw a punch, a fist like a wooden mallet hitting Gallant high on the head. But the punch lacked strength, lacked speed. And now Tancred's eyes were rolling, the lids fluttering.

Gallant's shot had hit him under the heart. He had been fighting on will power and instinct. But life had drained away with the hot blood that pulsed from the wound. He flopped away from Gallant, gasping like a landed fish. His thick fingers opened and closed, muscular spasms beyond his control. Then his breath rasped in his throat, rattled – and he was still.

Gallant shook his head. He climbed to his feet, swayed. Slid the Peacemaker back into his waistband.

Rubbed his shoulder.

'Impressive performance,' Mack Flynn said, 'but all to no avail.'

He stepped away from the smashed timber and sprung barrels that were all that remained of the bar, glass crunching under his boots. He'd picked up the briefcase. It dangled carelessly from one hand. In the other he was holding a six-gun.

'What I'm about to do now should have been done at the outset,' he said. 'If there's trouble, you don't watch it develop, you eliminate it. Why couldn't Wakeman understand that simple fact?'

Without pause, he lifted the six-gun, drew back the hammer.

The double crack of the two shots was impossible to separate.

Flynn stood frozen. His arm was raised. The six-gun held steady on Gallant's face – but the trigger had not been pulled, the hammer had not fallen. Two black holes appeared in the centre of the Texan's chest. One inch apart. Then, as if a balloon had been pricked, he seemed to fold in on himself. A young man withered and became old, and then even age was something in his past. He died on his feet, went down in a crumpled heap and toppled sideways to lie across the body of Sundown Tancred.

'You wouldn't let me come in with you, and almost paid the price,' Melody Lake said breathlessly, clutching Gallant's arm and shaking it as she ran to him out of the shadows. 'I was horrified. Flynn came strutting out of the back room, and you were tangled up with that big 'breed. You needed help, but a wild shot might have killed you by mistake.'

'Sundown Tancred was a hard man to put down, and Flynn caught me cold,' Gallant said. 'But who the hell—?'

And then, as another figure carrying a gleaming .73 Winchester scuffed his way through the sawdust into the weak circle of light, Gallant grinned ruefully through his pain.

'Stick McCrae,' he said. 'So you're the horseman I heard. I might have known if there was a story to be sniffed out it would be you doing the sniffing.'

'I frequently find myself wondering why I go to such lengths for a scoop,' McCrae said, 'though this is the first time I've had to help kill a man for my copy.'

'But perhaps not the last,' Gallant said. 'The story's not finished, Stick.'

'It may not be finished,' Melody said, 'but the hard work's done, the worst of it over. Three smug ranchers are sitting at the Taylor spread, and they'll still be sitting there smoking their cigars and drinking to a job well done when we ride into the Rocking L and hand those papers to my pa.'

'And after that?'

'Kansas City.' She smiled at him, her eyes dancing. 'And then, with the convention over and Consolidated legally brought into being, if I know Stick McCrae we'll both be reading our names in the *Kansas City Star*.'

'Famous partnerships,' Gallant said, 'have been

formed from far less promising beginnings.'

For a brief moment Melody looked steadily into his clear blue eyes. Then, with a thoughtful pout and an enigmatic shake of the head, she turned away from him and started out of the Last Chance saloon.

AUTHOR'S NOTE

This story is loosely based on historical fact. In 1884 the National Cattle Growers' Association was formed in Chicago, and the same year saw the formation of the National Cattle and Horse Growers Association of the United States. In 1885 the two associations were merged to form the Consolidated Cattle Growers Association of the United States. The organization was short lived. In 1887, after the worst winter ever recorded, Consolidated faded away.

While this story is based on those incidents, locations have been tinkered with, and none of the characters here portrayed ever existed in real life.